This Present Darkness
Piercing the Darkness
Prophet
Tilly

THE COOPER KIDS ADVENTURE SERIES
The Door in the Dragon's Throat
Escape from the Island of Aquarius
The Tombs of Anak
Trapped at the Bottom of the Sea

ESCAPE FROM THE ISLAND OF AQUARIUS

FRANK E. PERETTI

CROSSWAY BOOKS
WHEATON, ILLINOIS

Escape from the Island of Aquarius

Copyright © 1986 by Frank E. Peretti

Published by Crossway Books
        a publishing ministry of Good News Publishers
        1300 Crescent Street
        Wheaton, Illinois 60187

Cover design: The DesignWorks Group,
        www.designworksgroup.com

Cover photo: Steve Gardner

www.perettionline.com

Printed in the United States of America

Library of Congress Catalog Card Number 85-72915

ISBN 13: 978-1-58134-619-0
ISBN 10: 1-58134-619-0

BP		15	14	13	12	11	10	09	08	07
15	14	13	12	11	10	9	8	7	6	5	4

*To the kids
at Camp L.I.F.E.
1985*

ONE

It was a hot, clear day on the South Pacific, and the ocean had that slow, lazy feel that could rock you to sleep with its gently rolling swells. The captain of the chugging trawler was bored and playing checkers with his first mate while another crewman stayed at the ship's wheel. There wasn't much to talk about, so nobody did much talking. They had hauled in their catch and were headed for port, and that was all that mattered.

Then the crewman at the wheel yelled, "Hey, Cap! There's something off the port bow!"

"I've seen it," the captain said dryly. "I've seen everything."

The first mate stood to look, as did other men here and there on the boat.

"You haven't seen this," said the first mate.

"I'll wager I have," said the captain, getting up from the checker game, "and now I'll see it one more time, and you'll not be at any advantage for being away from our game, mark my words! I've—"

The words stopped short in the captain's mouth. Something *was* out there.

"One quarter ahead," he said finally. "Rudder to port. We'll heave to."

The tired and rusty trawler turned lazily to the left and pushed slowly through the water, getting closer to what looked like a tangle of boards and driftwood.

Through binoculars, the captain saw it clearly. There, out in the middle of absolutely nowhere, floated a very small, battered, wave-washed raft made of boards, logs, trees, rags, anything. In the middle of the raft, lashed to one bleached and bent mast, was a man. He was not moving.

"Easy now," said the captain, and the engines shut down completely. A ladder was lowered over the side, and two crewmen clambered down it. They dangled from the ladder by one hand and one leg and let the blue-green, foaming water pass slowly under them. Then, when the little raft came slowly by, one dropped onto it and caught a rope tossed by the other. The raft was quickly secured to the trawler.

But the report was not good.

"He's dead, Cap!" the crewman shouted, his voice tinged with disgust.

"We'll have a look at him," ordered the captain over the rail.

They hauled the body on board. It was cold and stiff, and the clothing was ragged.

"Looks like a native of one of the islands near here," said the first mate.

"Ehhh . . ." said the captain thoughtfully, examining a strange medallion around the man's neck. "And I know which one."

They all took a look at the heavy copper medallion. It bore a symbol of the zodiac.

"Aquarius," said the captain.

"There really is such a place?" a crewman asked.

"Whether or not you want to believe it," the captain answered.

The first mate suddenly bent to look at the man's

feet. The expression on his face made all the others follow suit.

"The hairs are singed," said one.

"Yeah, Aquarius it is for sure," the first mate agreed.

"Then a legend, a rumor, a tall tale has fallen right into our laps," the captain said, "and now I'll wager it wasn't the sea that killed him."

"Then what did?" a crewman asked.

"Whether or not you want to believe it," said the captain in a low voice, his eyes glued on the dead man, "it could have been a curse . . . or a spirit . . . something dark, and altogether unkind. Look, you can see it in his face." Then he ordered, "Check the pockets. And check that raft. Let's see who he is."

Someone found a little scrap of paper, like a note, in the man's shirt pocket.

"Mighty washed out," said the finder.

"Any name on it?" the captain asked, taking a look himself.

The crewman squinted and turned the little paper this way and that. "Looks like some missionary outfit . . . 'International Missionary Alliance' . . . Ah! Here's a name . . . Adam . . . Mac . . . MacKenzie?"

The captain had a look. "So it is. And Sacramento, it looks like." He looked at the dead man. "This is not MacKenzie, I'm sure. But we'll take him to Samoa and let the powers-that-be have their talk with these missionary people or this Mr. MacKenzie. That'll be the end of our part in this."

Dr. Jake Cooper sat in the back of the little cruiser as it putt-putted across the blue water, his sharp eyes constantly checking the horizon and then referring to the map laid out in front of him. He removed his wide-brimmed hat, wiped sweat from his brow, and looked at his watch.

"It's been fifty-five minutes," he said.

His fourteen-year-old son, Jay, kept a strong and steady hand on the helm and his eyes on the boat's compass.

"Well, Dad," he said, looking again to be sure, "I still don't see any island out there."

Jay's sister, Lila, thirteen, sat on a cushion to one side, her head hanging over the rail, her blonde hair hanging over her glazed eyes.

"Land . . . land . . ." she pleaded.

"It's got to be there!" Dr. Cooper exclaimed, picking up his binoculars.

"Why?" ask Lila. "We've been to twenty different islands now and nobody we've talked to has even heard of an island called Aquarius."

"Not by that name, no," Dr. Cooper answered, peering across the water through the binoculars. "But all the natives and tribes around here seem to know the rumors about some island that is taboo, or cursed, or evil. The very fact that they refuse to talk about it is strong evidence for its existence."

"Well," Jay said, "I just hope that tribal chief back at the last island was right. So far I don't see a thing."

"We still have time. He said it was about an hour north, but . . . well, he could have been mistaken about the distance." Dr. Cooper looked at Lila again. "Don't worry, Lila. Whether or not it's Aquarius, we'll spend the night there and give you a chance to be on steady ground again."

"All this over a little note," she muttered sickly.

"Well," said Dr. Cooper, "the International Missionary Alliance seemed to think that little note was a vital link to MacKenzie. He disappeared in this area and was assumed dead over two years ago, remember, but now this note turns up in the pocket of a dead man, and the handwriting is definitely MacKenzie's."

"Which means he could still be alive somewhere," said Jay.

"But why did the Alliance hire us to find him?" Lila wondered.

Dr. Cooper couldn't help getting a twinkle in his eye. "Well, under the circumstances, I don't think anyone else wanted the job."

"Under the circumstances . . ." Lila thought aloud. "A spooky island everyone's afraid of and a dead man with no good reason to be dead!"

"That last part does have me perplexed," said Dr. Cooper. "That man's death was far from normal. I talked to the authorities in Samoa, but all they could give me was guesses about poisons and rumors about Aquarius, and that medallion around his neck. I'm afraid we'll have to find out everything else for ourselves."

"I thought we were archaeologists," Lila said.

"We're also very good at snooping," Jay said playfully.

Lila had to shrug and nod in agreement.

"MacKenzie's note—what there was of it—seemed to be a cry for help," their father remarked, digging a photocopy of the note from his briefcase. "But as many times as I look at it, I can't make anymore of it out."

"Let me see it again," Lila asked.

Dr. Cooper handed the copy to her, and she studied it for a long, curious moment before shaking her head.

"I see what you mean," she said. "All I can read is 'come quickly, the island is' . . . uh . . . 'the island is . . .' "

"The island is dead ahead!" exclaimed Jay.

Dr. Cooper grabbed up the binoculars. He broke into a grin.

"Yes!" he said. "I can see that rocky promontory on the east end, just as the chief described it."

Now Lila wasn't feeling quite so sick, and she stood beside Jay and waited for her turn with the binoculars. When she got her first look, she said, "Wow! It looks like the loneliest place in the world. I don't think *I'd* want to be a missionary there."

"Missionaries are a special breed," said Dr. Cooper. "When God calls them, they go, no matter where. Somebody has to get the gospel to . . . the loneliest place in the world."

"More power to them," said Jay.

"Well . . . if God said so, I guess I'd go," said Lila.

"That's what Adam MacKenzie did," Dr. Cooper answered. "Now let's hope we find him alive and well."

The little cruiser took another forty-five minutes to approach the island, and the Coopers watched with curiosity as the faint line of dark green on the horizon came closer, growing into an expansive island with thick vegetation, waving palm trees, and towering, jagged rocks.

"Hmmm . . ." Dr. Cooper mused. "Volcanically formed, unlike the coral islands around here. Watch for reefs. They have a way of sneaking up on you."

"Get a load of those," said Jay, pointing to some very jagged rocks that stuck up above the water like sawteeth.

"Are there any rumors about this island eating boats?" Lila asked.

"No, just people," said her father. "They say that no one ever returns from here."

Jay slowed the cruiser to a very cautious crawl. Lila perched on the bow to look out for the rocks that crouched just under the surface. They moved slowly along through the water in the red light of the setting sun, looking for a safe way to reach the white sanded beach.

When the water became shallow, they could see the bottom—rocky, rugged, treacherous, but very beautiful with countless shells, pink and crimson coral, and huge schools of tiny, fiery fish that darted away with one mind as the boat passed over them.

Jay steered the boat along the shoreline for a short while, and finally they came to a small cove that looked very inviting. They pulled into it just as the sun dipped below the distant, glassy-smooth horizon. Lila dropped the anchor, Jay turned off the little engine, and all was quiet. The three of them sat in the growing darkness for a long time, watching and listening.

"I guess everything's normal enough," Lila said very softly.

She felt Dr. Cooper's gentle hand on her shoulder.

"Maybe not," he said quietly, pointing. "Look at those palms over there, that whole grove."

The three looked. Over to one side of the cove, now silhouetted against the red sky, a very large grove of palm trees grew out of the ocean, as if swamped by a very high tide. But there was no high tide.

"I don't get it," said Jay.

"Mm, we'll just keep it in mind," said Dr. Cooper.

"Wait!" Lila hissed. "Listen!"

Rustle. Rustle. Swish. Crack. Something was moving through the thick brush near the shore. Dr. Cooper reached for the spotlight on the top of the cruiser and clicked it on. The powerful beam shot across the shallow water of the cove, spotlighting the trees and the thick, green vegetation.

Rustle. Crackle. The sound moved haltingly, stopping, going, stopping again. Dr. Cooper followed it with the light, the big beam swinging slowly sideways.

There! For just a moment, some thick, low-growing leaves rustled and quivered. Then a bush shook nervously.

The big spot of light moved slowly along, illuminating big circles of plant life, trees, and rocks.

A face!

It was like a fright mask in some carnival fun house; with wide and wild eyes, a gray, scraggly beard, and jagged teeth that glistened in the beam of the spotlight.

The thing, or creature, or person, jumped out of the bushes and began to wave its skinny arms, hollering, "No! Go away! Go *away*, you!"

"Is this Aquarius?" Dr. Cooper shouted.

But the anxious little character suddenly spotted something alarming. He let out a frightened squawk and immediately vanished into the bushes.

Dr. Cooper swept the big light back and forth, calling, "Are you there? Hello?"

There was no answer from the silent shore.

"Something spooked him," Jay said.

"Yeah, but what?" Lila wondered.

"Oh-oh! Look over there!"

They all saw it. A light was moving through the jungle, coming their way.

Dr. Cooper reached for his 357 revolver and buckled it on. "We're in for a reception," he said.

The light bobbed steadily toward them, blinking behind the trees, branches, and bushes. Finally it broke into the open and moved along the shore, floating about seven feet above the ground.

"Is . . . is that—" Jay began to ask.

"Yes," said Dr. Cooper, peering into the darkness. "I believe it's exactly what it looks like."

"How does he do that?" Lila asked.

The light was from some kind of torch, which rested on, or rather was stuck to, the top of a very tall

Polynesian's bald head. The man stood on the shore looking out at them, a scowl on his dark face, his arms at his sides, his body straight and clothed in skins, bones and grass. He looked like a tall, muscular candle.

The Coopers could only stare at him and then at each other.

"I think," said Dr. Cooper, "we've found the right place."

The Polynesian's deep voice boomed across the still water. "You! Who you?"

Dr. Cooper called, "We are the Coopers from the United States. We're looking for a missionary named Adam MacKenzie!"

The man's big eyes widened, and his bronze chest swelled with a long, slow gasp of either horror or delight.

"You!" he roared. "You come! You come!"

The Coopers exchanged glances, and all three had expressions on their faces that said, "I sure don't know about this!"

The man fired some unintelligible native words at them, his big arms waving like a windmill. He closed with, "Come! Come plenty now, don't afraid!"

"Well . . ." Dr. Cooper said quietly to Jay and Lila, "he's civilized to the extent of some English."

"In other words, we're going to go ashore," said Jay.

"We'll carry standard provisions," Dr. Cooper instructed. "I don't plan to be away from the boat for very long, especially with all the explosives we have on board."

"Jay," asked Lila teasingly, "just why did you bring all that blasting equipment along? This isn't an archaeological dig, it's a weird little island."

Jay shrugged. "Ehhh, force of habit, I guess."

"Maybe we'll need to open some coconuts," said Dr. Cooper.

They all laughed at that and gathered their gear together while the big torchman on the beach stood and watched.

"Stick close together," Dr. Cooper said.

With packs on their backs and lights in their hands, they stepped into the clear, shallow water and waded to shore. The Polynesian was even bigger up close, but around his neck hung something that riveted their attention: a copper medallion with the sign of Aquarius.

TWO

The big man turned a slow, silent turn, rolled his eyes toward the jungle, and started walking back the way he had come.

Dr. Cooper let Jay and Lila go ahead so he could keep watch from the rear, and away they went in single file. The primitive trail meandered through heavy growth, passed under huge fallen trees, through hurrying streams, and up rocky grades. The air in the deep forest was warm and wet. Darkness and an ominous silence surrounded them as they followed that big man with the bright burning torch upon his head, the torch casting long shadows that danced far back among the trees.

After a while they began trudging up a steep grade, and could feel sharp, broken rocks under their feet. The vegetation started to thin out as they climbed higher, and finally the bright silver light of the moon broke through the thinning treetops. The ground all around became a moonscape, a barren mountaintop of rock. They climbed higher.

A new sound met their ears. From somewhere came a deep, throaty, gargling roar of water.

Now they were moving along a narrow, rocky ridge. On one side the ground dropped off into a bottomless, black chasm, and far, far below was that fierce and angry water.

Their guide took a small turn toward the chasm, stepped down onto something, and then the light from the torch began to bob up and down, up and down like a walking yo-yo.

Lila broke the silence. "Oh, no! I can't go over that!"

The man did not seem to hear her, but continued walking across the most precarious, flimsy, rubbery suspension bridge any of them had ever seen. His big feet played a tune on the weathered planks, and his body rose and fell as the primitive and fraying ropes stretched and pulled, sagged and tightened, stretched and pulled, sagged and tightened.

Lila ventured onto the bridge, holding the rope rails for dear life and feeling seasick again. "Lord, please don't let me fall!" she prayed aloud.

Dr. Cooper waited for the guide and Lila to reach the other side before allowing Jay to try for it. In the meantime he peered down into the chasm, listening to the roar of the water.

"Tell me, Jay," he said. "Ever hear a river or a waterfall that sounded like that?"

Jay was happy enough to pause before tackling the bridge. He leaned over the chasm and listened.

The sound was very strange, not like the usual dashing, splashing sound of a river, and not like the usual crashing and thundering of a waterfall. It sounded like—like . . .

"What in the world is going on down there?" Jay finally asked.

It was too dark to tell.

"They say that Adam MacKenzie drowned, even though he was an excellent swimmer . . ." Dr. Cooper said thoughtfully.

Jay shined his light down into the chasm, but the beam was lost in the sheer distance. Even the moonlight was blocked by the deep shadows cast by the rocky cliffs. Below them lay nothing but darkness—darkness and that very strange, throaty, gargling roar.

The big guide was bellowing at them again, so Jay and Dr. Cooper hurriedly yo-yoed across the bridge, getting to the other side none too soon.

Not long after the bridge, they began to see lights up ahead and heard the sounds of a village: voices, some tools clattering, a few goats bleating.

They rounded a corner, and the trail became a road that led them into a rather quaint village of small cottages and bungalows with a definite, civilized, American flavor.

The homes were well-built, with durable slate roofs, front porches, and even a few porch swings. They had glass windows, hinged doors, real welcome mats, clotheslines, and electric lights. The Coopers saw people of all ages, working, playing, resting, talking. But these people were not Polynesians. They were civilized Westerners.

"Are you sure we haven't come ashore somewhere in Ohio?" Jay asked his father and sister.

Dr. Cooper was visibly surprised. "This is certainly not the kind of village I expected to find on a remote South Sea island. It must be some kind of . . . colony."

They passed one little house with a woman and two children sitting under the porchlight in the cool of the evening. The woman wore the now-familiar Aquarius medallion around her neck. Dr. Cooper waved and said hello. She waved back, but said nothing.

Three carpenters were relaxing around a small outdoor table and laughing loudly. When the Coopers came by the men immediately fell silent, staring vacantly as the strangers passed.

The Coopers said good evening, but again they got no answer. Identical copper medallions hung around each man's neck. Everybody seemed to wear them here, and everybody stared at the Coopers. Although the place looked like some quaint American suburb in paradise, it was clear that these people were not at all used to visitors.

The newcomers continued down the dirt street, passing more cottages, a small carpentry shop, a maintenance building, and then a large meeting hall. They finally came to a large, stately cottage facing the village square.

The big Polynesian stepped onto the veranda and rang a very loud brass ship's bell. Women, men, children, youths, and elders from all around the square began to gather, staring at the Coopers with great curiosity and a little grimness. After a short moment, the door of the cottage opened and a man stepped out. He spoke to the Polynesian and then turned his gaze on the three unknowns.

The Coopers used the time to observe the man. He was middle-aged, strong looking, with graying hair, piercing eyes, and a very impressive air of authority. A very ornate copper medallion dangled from his neck. He simply stood there, a cold expression on his face, studying them up and down for what seemed like the longest time before he finally spoke.

"Welcome to the Isle of Aquarius. Who are you, where do you come from, and what brings you here?"

Dr. Cooper answered, "We are Dr. Jake Cooper and his two children, Jay and Lila, of Cooper Incorporated, an archaeological research firm. We hail from the United States of America, and we are here on behalf of the International Missionary Alliance to search for a missing missionary, the Reverend Adam MacKenzie."

The man exchanged just the quickest little glance

with some of the gathered people and then he broke into a smile, something he had not seemed capable of.

"And what makes you think you'll find him here?" he asked.

Dr. Cooper reached into his shirt pocket and brought out a copper medallion. "I notice everyone here is wearing one of these. This was found on a man adrift in the middle of the ocean."

The slight smile on the man's face faded quickly as Dr. Cooper told about the dead man on the primitive raft.

"Can you describe him?" the man asked.

Dr. Cooper produced a photograph. Several people gathered to look at it, and then gasped and muttered.

"Tommy!" they said. "It's Tommy!"

The man looked at the picture and scowled, shaking his head.

"Tommy was our nickname for him," he said mournfully. "He was a very sweet person. We all loved him."

"Do you have any idea how he ended up adrift and dead in the middle of the ocean?" Dr. Cooper asked.

"He was alive when he left here on that raft," said the man, "but his death is certainly no surprise. It may be hard for you to understand, not having lived here in this place, but . . ." The man raised his voice as if he wanted all the people to hear. "There are very powerful energies still at work on this island, created by ancient traditions. The more primitive observer would call it—forgive me—magic. At any rate, we still encounter these forces from time to time, and one such manifestation is a terrible madness, an inescapable curse that sometimes besets people here. The native word is *Moro-Kunda;* it means the Madness Before Death. It has no known cause, no known cure, and is always fatal.

"This curse fell upon Tommy. He went mad, and

though we tried to stop him, he fabricated that crude raft and fled from the island." The man paused dramatically and then added, "But he couldn't escape Moro-Kunda."

All the people in the square gasped and muttered again. Every face was filled with horror and dismay.

"Well . . . be that as it may . . ." Dr. Cooper took a sheet of paper from his pack and handed it to the man. "This is a photocopy of a note found in Tommy's pocket. You'll notice the Sacramento address of the International Missionary Alliance at the top, and there, near the bottom, is the name Adam MacKenzie. The writing was all but obliterated by seawater, but what can be seen is definitely MacKenzie's handwriting. It seems to be a cry for help—"

Dr. Cooper stopped his explanation. The man had suddenly burst out laughing. As he looked at some of the people, they began laughing too.

"Sorry . . . sorry . . ." the man said, trying to control himself. "I know this must seem like a very serious matter to you."

"Well," Dr. Cooper tried to explain, "MacKenzie was thought to be dead. Drowned. But now this note could be proof that he's still alive somewhere . . ."

"Oh, he is definitely alive, Dr. Cooper!"

Dr. Cooper exchanged glances with Jay and Lila, and asked, "Then . . . you know this MacKenzie?"

"Quite well."

"Do you know where we can find him?"

"You have found him," said the man with a smile. "I am Adam MacKenzie!"

Lila chuckled. "Well, that was easy!"

But Dr. Cooper didn't know whether to smile or frown, whether to doubt or question or just accept this man's words.

"You are MacKenzie?" he finally asked.

The man stepped forward and offered his hand. "You can believe it, Doctor! I had no idea I was in such dire trouble, but I certainly thank you for coming to rescue me!"

He laughed again, and then looked at the people in the square, and they all laughed again.

"You see," said MacKenzie, "this note is something I must have written ages ago, and somehow it got misplaced. I was writing to the Alliance to tell them how well things were going."

"And those words, 'please come quickly, the island is . . .'?"

"I believe I wrote, 'Please come quickly, the island is the most beautiful place in the world!' I wanted them to come and visit us here, and see what we've been able to accomplish!" MacKenzie laughed again. "I always wondered why I never got an answer! I gave it to Tommy to send through the U.S. Post Office in Samoa. He must have forgotten, and was carrying it in his pocket all this time!"

Dr. Cooper forced a smile. "Well . . . I'm glad to find that you're all right."

"And not dead, I assure you!" said MacKenzie.

"The Alliance will be glad to hear that. They're certainly wondering whatever became of you. You haven't been heard from in over two years."

"As you can see all around you," MacKenzie said, "I've been very busy!"

The Coopers could see that, as Dr. Cooper had said, this was not the kind of village one would expect on a remote South Sea island.

"Surprising, isn't it?" MacKenzie asked with a chuckle. "Where one might expect a remote, untouched island with a very primitive culture at best, one finds instead a beautiful new world, a bold new civilization, a literal heaven on earth!" He turned to the big Polynesian. "Candle, take the Coopers' packs and belongings into the guest hut. They can stay with us tonight and get a fresh start back in the morning!"

Candle lifted all three of their packs in his big arms.

"Oh, and Candle . . ." said MacKenzie, "I think you can extinguish that thing now."

Candle took a tall hat from his belt and put it on, snuffing out the torch. Then he carried the Coopers' packs to a small little bungalow that faced the square.

"He's still rather primitive," explained MacKenzie. "Even though we now produce our own electricity, he can't give up his old, traditional means of lighting his way. Oh, and Doctor . . ." MacKenzie gave Dr. Cooper's gun a raised eyebrow. "If our people seem a little alarmed at your presence, it could be because of your weapon. We have no weapons here. This is an island of perfect peace."

Dr. Cooper smiled and spoke not only to MacKenzie, but to anyone else within earshot. "Don't worry. I carry it only for protection."

"Which won't be necessary here, I assure you," said MacKenzie.

Dr. Cooper only nodded, and then asked, "And just who are all these people? Where have they come from?"

MacKenzie looked around the square, pointing out particular faces as he said, "These are people from all walks of life, from lawyers to doctors, from carpenters to college professors. They came from America, from Great Britain and Australia. Some are from France and Germany. All share in our dream, Doctor."

"Which is?"

"Our own brand-new world, a place free from crime, war, bloodshed, and greed. We've left the old world behind, we've escaped the rat race, and now we are building a new world for ourselves. Let me show you around!"

MacKenzie gave them a tour of the village, from one end to the other.

"See here?" he said, pointing this way and that. "We have our own water system, sewer system, and electric power. It took years of backbreaking work, but we accomplished it." They walked further. "Here's our woodshop where we build whatever we need, whether new carts for hauling wood or new kitchen cabinets or toys for the children. And this is our community kitchen where our skilled cooks prepare all our meals . . ."

The tour lasted a long time.

"So," Dr. Cooper ventured to ask, "what you've done here is start your own society, all over again, beginning from scratch?"

"Exactly! That is the theme of our group medallion you've seen us all wearing. The sign of Aquarius is an international symbol of a coming age of world peace. We are realizing that right here, right now."

"And where is your church?"

"Oh . . ." MacKenzie hesitated, and then answered, "The meeting hall. You passed it on your way in, remember? We meet there to discuss spiritual matters."

"Mm-hmm," said Dr. Cooper thoughtfully.

Jay noticed a wide path turning off into the jungle and walked toward it for a closer look. "Where does this go?"

MacKenzie looked strangely alarmed. "Oh, don't go that way!"

Jay stopped short and stared at MacKenzie in bewilderment.

MacKenzie explained, "That's—well, that goes into the jungle, but it—it really isn't safe out there. I need to tell all of you not to venture away from the village."

"Why?" asked Jay. "What's out there?"

"Uh . . . well . . ." MacKenzie hesitated in answering. "We don't know, really. But some strange things have happened lately, and we just think that it would be safer to remain in the village. There's something evil out there . . . something dangerous."

"Are you talking about another curse, or power, like the Moro-Kunda?" asked Dr. Cooper.

"Perhaps," said MacKenzie. "This is a different part of the world, Dr. Cooper. There are powers, forces, ancient traditions here that are still beyond our understanding."

"But surely a man of God like yourself would know that there are only two sources of such things: supernatural occurrences are either from God or from Satan. There's really nothing very mysterious about it."

MacKenzie chuckled. "Doctor, there is much that you do not yet know. Beware of old religious prejudices and ignorance. They can be your greatest enemy. That is why Jesus came to earth, to save us from our ignorance, isn't that so?"

"Since you ask," said Dr. Cooper, "no, it is not so."

MacKenzie only smiled. They walked further, and he continued to chat, but all three Coopers felt a growing uneasiness about this man and place.

And Jay kept hearing a sneaking, stealthy rustling just a short distance behind them. MacKenzie was too busy talking to hear it, and Lila and Dr. Cooper seemed to be too far ahead. But to Jay, lagging just a little behind, it sounded much like the noise they had heard at the cove.

What was that? He stopped walking just long enough to listen. It was breathing. Deep, heavy breathing. And then some moaning.

Jay hurried his steps and caught up with the rest of the group.

Just then a distinguished-looking gentleman came

out of one of the houses and called to MacKenzie.

"Hello!" he said. "I'm glad I caught you!"

MacKenzie hurried toward the man, blurting out words with an explosive abruptness. "Bert! Bert, how's it going? I want you to meet some visitors! They came looking for Adam MacKenzie, and imagine their surprise when they found out it was *me!*"

"Oh . . ." Bert said, and then he looked at the Coopers and laughed. "Oh, yes!"

"Dr. Cooper, Jay, Lila, this is Bert Hammond, our resident physician. He mends the cuts, sets the fractures, and delivers the babies, right, Bert?"

"Yes, that's right," said Bert. He added to MacKenzie, "Say, I was wondering if you'd like to come in and check those supply inventories. We still have some items missing."

"Of course, of course," said MacKenzie. He turned to the Coopers and said, "Could you please wait just a moment for me? Don't stray away. I'll be right back."

With that, the two men went into the house.

"Why do I feel so funny about all this?" Lila asked very quietly.

"I hope you two have been observing everything," Dr. Cooper said.

"*I'm* observing something right now," said Jay. "We're being followed!"

"I know," said Dr. Cooper. "It could be that same character we saw at the cove."

"Then you've heard it too?"

"As much as I've been able, with all of MacKenzie's chattering."

Suddenly a very eerie voice called from the jungle a short distance behind them, "Hellooooo . . . strangers! Visitors! Over here!"

"Never a dull moment . . ." said Dr. Cooper. "Stay close behind me. Jay, watch for MacKenzie."

They began to walk very quietly and slowly toward the edge of the jungle where they could now hear that deep, panting breath behind the bushes.

"Show yourself," said Dr. Cooper. "We'll talk."

Two very thick leaves parted, and there, not nearly so frightening this time, was that same wild-eyed, bearded face.

"Your name is Cooper?" the man asked, his big eyes glimmering in the dark.

"That's right. And yours?" asked Dr. Cooper.

A bony hand shot out. "Amos Dulaney, former professor of geology at Stanford." All three Cooper mouths opened, but Dulaney blurted, "Please, no questions! Just listen. You *must* get away from this island immediately! And please, take me with you. We can leave tonight. I can meet you back at the cove."

"You'll have to explain yourself."

"No time! I'll explain later! I—aaawww!"

The Coopers ducked. The 357 was in Dr. Cooper's hand in an instant. Something had grabbed Dulaney and he disappeared behind the bushes, screaming and struggling.

"Let go!" he screamed. "Let me go!"

Dr. Cooper moved in to help, but suddenly a huge man burst out of the jungle like an angry elephant, holding the thrashing, wriggling Dulaney around the waist and carrying him into the clearing.

"Stay out of this!" the man ordered.

"Help me!" screamed Dulaney. "Don't let him do this to me!"

The ruckus could be heard all over the village. Doors burst open and men came running, many with guns and rifles. There were shouts, orders, and then more men.

The Coopers could only stand and watch, dumbfounded.

THREE

MacKenzie burst out of Bert Hammond's home and came running.

"Hold him!" he ordered.

"Aaawww! No! No!" Dulaney screamed.

"Get back!" another man ordered the Coopers.

They backed away.

MacKenzie ran up to the struggling mass of men and took one quick look at Dulaney.

Then he backed away, his hands outstretched toward the kicking, wiggling man, his eyes wide with horror.

"Moro-Kunda!" he shouted.

It was incredible! As if Dulaney were a hot coal or a bomb about to explode, all those powerful men—at least a dozen of the village's strongest and burliest—dropped him on the ground and scattered in all directions. When they had retreated to what must have been a safe distance, they aimed their guns at Dulaney and surrounded the screaming man with a very wide circle.

"Get away!" MacKenzie yelled at the Coopers. "Get away! This man is cursed!"

"Let's do as he says," Dr. Cooper advised, and the three of them hurried into the yard of a nearby home where they stood and watched.

Dulaney, cowering now in the middle of that wide, heavily armed circle, screamed, "Don't listen to him! It's a lie!"

"Be quiet!" MacKenzie ordered.

"This island is doomed!" Dulaney shouted. "All the animals and birds have fled, the tides are flooding the lowlands, the quakes are getting more and more severe—"

"I said be quiet!" MacKenzie shouted. Then, to some of the men, "Tom and Andrew, bring protectors! Move it!"

"Do you hear me?" Dulaney continued. "Get away from this island while you can! Kelno is lying to you!"

Tom and Andrew came running with what looked like several red scarves. They tossed the scarves to their comrades and every man whipped his scarf about his neck. Then, as if by magic, all the men grew brave again and moved in to take firm hold of Dulaney.

"Take him away!" MacKenzie ordered.

The guards carried the struggling, screaming Dulaney away.

MacKenzie seemed shaken. He turned to the Coopers very apologetically.

"As I said," he almost whispered, "this is a different part of the world. There are many things beyond our understanding."

Dr. Cooper walked right up to MacKenzie.

"I'd like to have all that explained to me," he said very firmly.

"Moro-Kunda—"

"I want more than that!" Dr. Cooper snapped.

"I can't tell you any more!" MacKenzie replied. "What do you want me to say? It isn't a disease, it isn't an infection . . . it's . . . it's an evil, a madness, an invisible, creeping curse that gets into a man who sets foot in the wrong places, or tampers with objects that are sacred, or defies the powers that rule here."

"You're supposed to be a missionary of the gospel of Jesus Christ," said Dr. Cooper, his eyes burning. "Tonight you're sounding more like a witch doctor! Now if it's a disease call it a disease, if it's insanity call it insanity, but don't expect me to accept some vague, unknowable trick of pagan medicine!"

MacKenzie's eyes grew very cold. "Once I believed as you do, but I have learned much on this island. There are many things you do not understand, Doctor . . ."

"Then enlighten me."

MacKenzie glared with growing anger at Jake Cooper. "Mark my words, good doctor! That man was once a very prominent and intelligent college professor and an upstanding member of this brave community! Now he's a raving madman, with delusions of doom, and I assure you that by tomorrow morning he will be dead! I've seen it happen before. I know what to expect."

"Dead from some *curse?*"

"The forces that rule this island cannot be challenged or opposed. To do so . . . brings Moro-Kunda."

Dr. Cooper pointed his finger right in MacKenzie's face, and his volume steadily rose. "Have you forgotten the power of the cross? Have you forgotten the Lordship of Jesus Christ over any tricks of Satan? You don't need to bow to this!"

"Nothing can violate the spirits that rule here," said MacKenzie. "Not even the gospel of Jesus Christ!"

Dr. Cooper was speechless.

MacKenzie only gestured to the Coopers to follow him. "I'll see that you're made comfortable. You can leave in the morning."

* * *

The guest hut was comfortable and warm, and the beds looked soft and pleasant.

But the Coopers did not feel comfortable.

Dr. Cooper remained by the door, his gun still hanging on his hip. He was wide-awake.

Jay was looking out the window toward the jungle. Lila sat by the other window, listening for a sound, any sound.

"Something is desperately wrong here," Dr. Cooper whispered.

"Moro-Kunda!" Lila said in disgust. "What kind of goofy game is MacKenzie playing?"

"I really didn't see that much wrong with Dulaney," her father stated.

"Are you sure?" asked Jay. "He seemed pretty wild to me."

"But remember what he said about the tides overflowing the lowlands? We saw that ourselves."

Lila brightened with recollection. "Those palm trees near the cove!"

"Right. And how about what Dulaney said about the wildlife? We haven't heard a bird or seen any sign of animals."

"Boy," said Jay, "on all the other islands we've visited, the noise in the jungle can keep you awake all night!"

"And MacKenzie himself . . ." Dr. Cooper said thoughtfully. "For a minister of the gospel he has some very strange ideas."

"Like Jesus coming to earth to save us from our ignorance?" asked Jay.

"Jesus didn't come to save us from ignorance," Lila exclaimed. "He came to save us from our *sin!*"

"And how about not even having a church in this village?" said Jay. "All they have is that meeting hall where they discuss spiritual matters! He showed us around in there, and I didn't see a Bible anywhere."

"Or a cross," added Dr. Cooper, "and I didn't hear him once mention prayer, or worship, or the reading of the Word."

"Some missionary!" said Lila.

"And did you hear him say he wrote that note ages ago? He must not have noticed the date on it. It was written six weeks ago!"

"He said they have no weapons here," said Jay, "but they sure had plenty of guns when Dulaney needed locking up!"

"And all that talk about building a new world for themselves," said Dr. Cooper, "and a coming age of world peace. He mentioned Aquarius, but I didn't hear him say that Christ's return would have anything to do with it."

"What was it Dulaney called MacKenzie?" asked Lila.

"Kelno," answered Dr. Cooper. "Whatever that means."

"So what were all those red scarves for? How do you stop germs with red scarves?"

"You don't stop germs. You stop . . . curses, or evil spirits, or forces, or whatever MacKenzie wants to call them. It's part of his game. The scarves—'protectors,' he called them. Like amulets, or trinkets, or good luck charms. It's witchcraft, pure and simple. It's all very wrong."

"Dad!" Jay whispered excitedly. "Look at this."

Dr. Cooper and Lila joined him at the window.

"Kill that light!" said Dr. Cooper, and Lila clicked it off.

They stood in the dark, peering out into the black, silent jungle.

In the distance, twinkling and blinking as it passed among the trees and vines, a floating, bobbing point of light moved silently along, the only thing visible.

"Candle . . ." said Jay.

"What's he doing out there at this time of night?" Lila asked.

"Wait a minute," said Dr. Cooper. "Jay, open the window a little more."

Jay cranked the window open. They all stood silently, hardly breathing.

They could hear it now. A kind of chanting, and wailing, and every once in a while a choruslike cheer. The effect was eerie.

"Are they having a party out there?" Jay asked.

"Out there, where it's supposed to be so dangerous, where there's supposed to be something evil lurking about . . ." Dr. Cooper mused. He listened for a while, then drew a deep breath and said, "Anybody here want to go for a hike?"

"What?" said Lila in horror.

"All right!" said Jay.

They took dark clothes from their packs and slipped into them, then picked up their lights, but did not turn them on. They gathered by the door to listen. The little village was so quiet it seemed deserted. The strange sounds from the jungle continued.

"That tree," whispered Dr. Cooper, and one by one—first Jay, then Lila, then Dr. Cooper—they dashed across the dimly-lit street and into the concealing shadow of a large palm.

"That grove over there," their father instructed, and one by one they dashed again.

With a few more silent, stealthy dashes, they worked their way back along the deserted dirt street to that forbidden trail Jay had found earlier.

"Now," said Dr. Cooper, "we'll find out whatever it is MacKenzie doesn't want us to know."

They moved down the trail, leaving the village lights behind and penetrating deeper and deeper into the wet, confining darkness of the jungle. From somewhere far ahead they still heard the eerie wailings and moanings of many voices. They clicked on their lights and aimed the beams low as they made their way steadily along.

The ground was soft with moss and humus. Except for an occasional squishing, their feet didn't make a sound. Above them, like black, slimy fingers, unseen vines hung down and occasionally smeared their faces with water and goo. The trail became narrower and darker. Then it split.

"Oh great . . ." said Jay.

"We'll have to divide up," said Dr. Cooper. "Lila, you keep watch here and give us a signal if anyone comes from behind. Jay, go ahead and take the right fork; I'll take the left."

With their lights held low and their heads ducked down to avoid the slimy vines, Dr. Cooper and Jay hurried up the two trails.

Lila turned her light off and stood in the blackness. For some time she could hear the footsteps of her father and brother and catch the ebbing sounds of vines swishing and twigs cracking. Those voices, wherever and whatever they were, continued their wailings, moanings, and singsong chants.

Squish. Squish.

What am I standing in? Lila wondered. She shone her light at her feet. Yes, it was that same squishy moss. She moved to some firmer ground just a few feet away.

Squish.

What now? No, no moss here.

Squish. Squish.

Lila moved her own feet. They didn't make such a sound.

Squish.

She froze. From somewhere she could hear drops of water plop, plop, plopping on the broad leaves of a plant.

Squish, squish.

"Dad?" she whispered. "Is that you?"

Nothing.

Then—crack, squish.

"Jay? Come on, you guys, speak up!"

From somewhere, some vines stirred.

Lila clicked on her light, tracing a white shaft through the hanging mist. She looked up one trail, then up the other.

No sign of her father or brother.

Squish. It was behind her!

She swung around.

"Aaawwww!"

A sudden, night-piercing scream numbed Lila's ears and froze her nerves. Her light went tumbling end-over-end into the bushes and she was knocked to the ground, entangled in roots, vines, leaves, and tendrils.

Something had her by the legs! She grappled, kicked, clawed at the branches and roots. She cried out, but her scream was swallowed up by the soft, mossy ground.

She tried to kick again, but now her legs were caught tightly. Something heavy had her, pulling her, clamping onto her body, grasp upon grasp, inch upon inch.

FOUR

The black world entangled Lila until she felt she was being eaten up. She raised her head out of the moss and leaves, and screamed.

An eternity passed. The clawing and grasping continued, hanging on, clamping her down, digging into her. Then she heard a strange, whispered plea, ". . . help . . . me."

And then the clawing stopped. Silence. *What now? Dear Jesus, am I going to die?*

"Lila!" came a voice. She looked up and saw the beam of a flashlight.

"Dad!" she said weakly.

She saw another light. Jay was coming on the run. Now the beams of light shone all around her. The weight was snatched away very suddenly, and she looked up just in time to see her father heave something aside as if it were a rag doll. The gun came into view.

"Dad, wait!" Jay cautioned, touching his father.

Dr. Cooper stood poised over the still form on the ground, the barrel of his gun aimed and ready. Then, almost immediately, he relaxed and turned the barrel aside, letting out a long sigh of relief.

"I'm all right, son," he said.

Lila immediately found herself held and cradled by four loving arms.

"Are you all right, sweetheart?" Dr. Cooper wanted to know. "Do you have any injuries?"

"I don't know . . ." she said, still dazed with fear.

"Can you get up?" asked Jay.

Though she was weak and shaky, there was nothing wrong with her.

"I guess I'm all right," she said. "What—what was it? What happened?"

Dr. Cooper went over to where he had flung the thing and turned it over. They all shined their lights on it.

"Mr. Dulaney!" Lila exclaimed.

He was quite dead, his mouth still frozen in a scream, his eyes wide and gawking with horror.

Dr. Cooper knelt down next to the body. He carefully examined the eyes, the face, the mouth. He rolled open one shirt-sleeve and examined the skin on the arm.

Finally he said quietly, "So this is Moro-Kunda."

Jay stared at his father in fear. "You really think so, Dad?"

"The symptoms are the same found on Tommy, the man on the raft: a separation of the blood, severe dehydration, and a burning of the flesh and skin—madness, panic, bizarre behavior. The doctors in Samoa told me what to look for. Whatever this Moro-Kunda is, it's killed both these men."

Lila asked, "So what was he doing to me? He wasn't, you know, attacking me?"

"I would say he was panic-stricken, Lila, clinging to you as a drowning man would cling to his rescuer. He wasn't responsible for his actions."

Suddenly another beam of light shone from behind

them, and a familiar voice said, "So now you believe me, Doctor?"

It was Adam MacKenzie, with two of his men.

"I would say I am very impressed," said Dr. Cooper.

MacKenzie shined his light in all their faces as if he was looking for something.

"You are fortunate," he said. "The curse has not spread to any of you . . . yet." He chuckled just a little, and it had a strangely menacing tone. "May I suggest that you all return to the village and to your hut, and, please, no more lurking about in the jungle. I told you it isn't safe out here. My men will see to Dulaney's body."

Dr. Cooper ventured to say, "We were wondering what all those people were doing out in the jungle this time of night."

"Doctor," said MacKenzie with another sinister chuckle, "this island can do strange things to your senses. There is no one anywhere outside the village tonight."

"We heard voices!" said Jay.

"Oh yes, certainly," MacKenzie replied, and then added, "But, young Mr. Cooper, such things are heard here often, and I'm afraid . . . it doesn't mean anyone is actually there."

When the Coopers were inside their hut with the door closed, they immediately went to the window to listen. All was quiet now. The voices were gone.

For the rest of the night they slept in rotating shifts, with two hours to sleep and one hour to keep watch. During Dr. Cooper's hour of watch, he remained quiet and let Jay and Lila sleep, even though he saw that distant, twinkling, blinking point of light from atop

Candle's head moving methodically through the jungle, this way and then that way, like a ferry shuttling back and forth on a distant, night-blackened sea. . . .

Dr. Cooper awoke with a start. In an instant he knew the whereabouts and status of his children and all the gear, and then he relaxed. Lila was still asleep and Jay was sitting on his cot by the door, leaning with tired eyes against the wall. The early light of day came through the windows.

Dr. Cooper could hear MacKenzie speaking very vigorously in the square outside.

"What's going on out there?" he asked.

"He's madder than a hornet," said Jay. "Some building materials are missing, and he's accusing everybody of being the thief."

"Oh?" said Dr. Cooper, joining his son by the door. "In this perfect world, free of crime and corruption, he has a thief?"

"Not for long, if he can help it. You ought to hear the threats he's shelling out. Wow!"

They both listened as MacKenzie bellowed and scolded from the veranda of his cottage.

". . . and never, never doubt this," they heard MacKenzie say, "this thief will be found! It will be far better for him to come forward now and confess than for me to find out for myself who he is, and even if I don't find out, the island knows and will reveal it to me! Someday, bold thief, you will see what it means to offend not only me and this village, but Aquarius itself! Then there will be no helping you."

"He's talking like this island's alive or something," Jay said.

Dr. Cooper only shook his head. "He's a real artist, isn't he?"

Lila stirred and sat up on her cot, her eyes squinting and her hair a mess.

"Whaz gon on?" she asked.

They explained it and let her listen to MacKenzie's ravings.

"We are now missing," said MacKenzie, "several board feet of lumber, two boxes of nails, ten tubes of caulking . . ." The list went to some length. "Now . . . I'll give you the rest of the day to think about it. If you are the thief, come to me and implore my mercy. If these items are returned, I'm sure the powers all around us will be merciful. If you continue in your stealth and your robbery, what can prevent your being cursed? What could even prevent . . . Moro-Kunda?"

Even from inside the hut, the Coopers could hear the people in the square responding to that same old threat with fearful muttering and whispering among themselves.

"Like puppets on a string!" said Dr. Cooper.

"They're really afraid of him, aren't they?" said Lila.

"That's how he controls them," said Dr. Cooper. "It's remarkable! Right out of the Bible!"

"Yeah," said Jay, "like in Second Thessalonians—that Scripture about the Antichrist deceiving everybody with power and signs and false wonders, right?"

"Remarkable!" Dr. Cooper couldn't help saying again. "It's just like a miniature antichrist's kingdom here, a miniature world dictatorship: one man ruling over everyone, everyone wearing his Aquarius medallion, and everyone afraid because of his great deceiving powers. It's almost a direct copy of Revelation 13!"

"But how in the world did a missionary of the gospel of Jesus Christ get so mixed up?" Jay wondered. "I mean, this guy is really off the wall!"

Dr. Cooper listened to MacKenzie boasting and

shouting in the village square, and then he thoughtfully shook his head.

"No," he said at last. "It isn't making sense. This man—if he is Adam MacKenzie—is most certainly very confused and very pitiful."

"So what are we going to tell the Missionary Alliance?" Lila wondered.

"We don't have enough information to tell them anything . . . yet," Dr. Cooper answered.

Adam MacKenzie very graciously and benevolently said good-bye to the Coopers. As a matter of fact, he almost seemed overjoyed and relieved to see them go. He quickly barked orders to Candle, who saw to it that soon all the Coopers' belongings were on their backs again and that they were more than ready to leave.

But MacKenzie did not stop there. He ordered Candle to escort the Coopers to their boat to be sure they did not get lost. As the Coopers saw it, he wanted to make very sure they were entirely successful in *leaving*.

With a firm handshake, MacKenzie bid them farewell and said, "I trust you have found your stay with us stimulating and challenging!"

"Oh, indeed we have," Dr. Cooper replied.

"And you will let the Alliance know that Adam MacKenzie is quite all right and accomplishing a great work here in the South Seas, won't you?"

"Why don't you write them and let them know yourself?" Dr. Cooper asked very pleasantly. "I'm sure they'd love to hear from you. As a matter of fact, you might make good on that invitation they never received, and send them another one. I'm sure they'd like to see in person what you're doing here."

"Yes! I'll do that," MacKenzie said, waving good-bye.

And I'll bet you won't, Dr. Cooper thought, as they left the village and headed through the jungle, followed by the tall, silent, and imposing Candle.

As they walked along, all three sent little visual signals to each other. They knew it could not end here. It would not be like them to just leave, and it certainly would not answer the many questions this whole trip had put in their minds. Sure, for now they would walk with Candle down to their boat, and they would probably even put out to sea—as long as Candle was watching.

But when they got to the boat—*then* they would talk things over.

Candle started shouting at them, but as usual they couldn't tell for sure what he was trying to say. They turned and looked back at him.

"You, you come!" he said, pointing off to the side of the trail.

Dr. Cooper stepped over to have a look. It was another trail, so small and obscured by the jungle that they had not even noticed it.

"Go!" said Candle, pointing down the trail.

Dr. Cooper tried to explain. "Candle, no, listen, this is not the way we came. We must return to the cove where our boat is anchored. Do you understand?"

Candle only knew that he wanted them to take this trail, and he kept pointing toward it in great earnest.

Jay and Lila looked at it, too. This little space between bushes did not look like it could go anywhere.

"He must have misunderstood his orders," Jay suggested.

Dr. Cooper nearly matched Candle's wide gestures as he explained, "We must go back the way we came . . . this way . . . *this* way, you understand?"

Candle looked frustrated. The Coopers continued walking down the main trail. Candle remained where he was, his face full of anger and despair. That was fine with the Coopers. They had had enough of being pushed, ordered, and escorted around this island.

But now they could hear that roar—that very strange roar—of water coming up out of the deep chasm spanned by that flimsy, precarious, possibly deadly excuse for a bridge. That bridge! To think they had actually crossed it in the dark! Here in the daylight, the ropes were clearly frayed and unraveling, decayed from years of changing seasons, salt air, rain, and sun. The boards forming the walkway had rotted to powder in many places, and many were missing, affording the traveler a sweeping view of certain death right under his feet.

Where was the *bottom* of that chasm? The Coopers craned their necks to find the point where the sheer rock walls finally met the river, or waterfall, or whatever was down there, but those walls just kept dropping and dropping like a huge, natural elevator shaft. Jay, consumed with curiosity, took several cautious steps out onto the bridge.

Then he grabbed the rope rails as his whole body stiffened and his eyes froze in a horrified stare.

"D—Dad!" he hollered, his voice shaking.

Dr. Cooper left the trail and went through the brush to step out onto a high ledge to one side of the bridge. He took his first look straight down into that chasm, and the expression on his face matched Jay's.

Lila stood right where she was. She had no desire at all to look.

Jay felt like he was looking into—into—

"It's like the biggest toilet in the world!" he shouted.

"That's not one bit funny!" Lila scolded.

Dr. Cooper had to chuckle to himself and admit

that Jay's observation was very descriptive. The chasm was several hundred feet across at its widest point, and the walls dropped sharply for a hundred feet or so to form an immense crater. It had to be an extinct volcanic crater, the main vent for the volcano that first formed the island. Now, with no more lava to spew forth, its throat was hollow and full of water, including the biggest, most ferocious, most thunderous whirlpool any human being had ever seen. The water churned, foamed, and raced around and around in a vast, deep-throated funnel shape; the very center of that funnel was a dark, bottomless, spinning hole that swirled with a continuous sucking roar which echoed and rumbled off the sheer walls.

Dr. Cooper hurried back to the bridge and signaled for Jay to head on across. Jay took a few moments to tear his eyes away from the incredible sight below him, and began to carefully choose each step across the bridge.

Lila was next. She stepped onto the bridge, but very hesitantly.

"Dad—" she started to say, but shut her lips tightly, grabbed the rope rails, and set out.

She moved out and away from solid ground with hesitant steps, crazily swaying and bobbing on that bridge like a drunken bird above the rocky cliffs.

And then there were no more cliffs, no more rocks, no more ground beneath her—only space, cold spray that hung in the huge crater, and what looked like a gargantuan mouth with white foaming lips and a bottomless black throat. Lila went numb.

"Go ahead, Lila," Dr. Cooper urged. "Just get it over!"

She forced herself to take another step.

The board crumbled! As her foot slipped through, she collapsed, grabbing onto the flimsy ropes, hanging on in stark terror. Below her, like little fluttering pine needles, the two halves of the board fell, drifted in the wind, shrank smaller and smaller, and almost became lost against the boiling, spinning texture of that angry mouth. Then they hit the water, and the monster whirlpool gobbled them up.

Lila couldn't move. The bridge kept heaving up and down, and she felt like it was trying to throw her off and cast her into that hungry monster. She peered with a frozen gaze into the abyss of turning water, and suddenly she was sure she was looking into a dizzying, rotating tunnel. *She* was the one turning. She couldn't think. She couldn't let go.

Then she felt her father's hand on her arm. She let him lift her, and she couldn't keep from clinging to him like a two-year-old as he carried her, one very careful step at a time, off that horrible bridge and back onto solid ground.

Dr. Cooper set Lila down, and she sank to the ground and sat there sheepishly.

"It's okay, honey," said Dr. Cooper.

Here came Jay, back across that bridge. *Jay, if you say one word, I'll bop you!* But he didn't mock her or chide her. He simply put his arms around her.

She started crying. "I'm sorry . . ."

"Hey, don't worry about it," said Jay.

"It happens," said her father.

"I've never had that happen to me before . . ." she whimpered. "I really lost it out there."

"Listen, I don't blame you," said Jay. "My heart's still in my throat!"

"Having that board break under you was all you needed!" Dr. Cooper said.

"I'm sorry," she said again, feeling her control returning. "But I don't think I can cross that thing!"

The three exchanged glances, and then the same thought hit all of them.

"That other trail . . ." said Dr. Cooper.

"Let's try it, *please*," said Lila.

"I'll bet Candle knew exactly what he was talking about," said Jay.

The new, unexplored trail wound down a steep hillside for quite a distance and then flattened out, taking the Coopers through thick jungle, working its way toward the sea. At first nothing unusual happened, and there were no obvious dangers.

Then Lila spotted something through the trees and slowed her walk.

"What's that over there?" she asked very quietly.

"A building of some kind . . ." Jay ventured.

It was a building, all right, a small grass hut. Beyond it was another hut, and beyond these two several more.

"Deserted," Dr. Cooper observed.

They checked the inside of the first hut. There could not have been much there to begin with, but something was not right about the emptiness of the little dwelling.

"Someone's been here," said Dr. Cooper, looking carefully at the ground. "Careful. See there? Footprints."

"With shoes," said Jay.

"Modern soles and heels," Dr. Cooper noted. "And look here. Several objects have been dragged out the door. Furniture, most likely."

Lila was looking at a primitive corral outside. The little fence had been broken down and the livestock was gone.

They found that the next hut had also been stripped bare of any tools, furniture, or valuables. A few broken and useless items lay here and there.

"I would say," said Dr. Cooper as he looked all around, "that this place has been looted. Someone's come here and carried everything off."

They moved further down the trail. Lila, ahead of Jay and Dr. Cooper, was the first to see the next shocking sight. She came to an abrupt halt on the trail and stood still there, looking with wide eyes, her hand over her mouth. The expression on her face brought Jay and Dr. Cooper on the run.

For the longest time, all three stood there speechless.

"I wonder if this is why Candle wanted us to come this way?" said Jay.

"Like he wanted us to see this," Lila added.

Below them lay an entire village of huts, animal shelters, corrals, and a lodge. The village was complete and appeared recently inhabited. As far as the Coopers could tell, there was only one thing wrong with it: It was half underwater.

"First those palm trees, and now this," said Dr. Cooper.

"Now we *know* something's wrong," Lila added.

"And so did Dulaney."

"And so did Tommy?" Jay asked.

"This village could have been lived in yesterday," said Dr. Cooper. "This extremely high tide is something very recent."

"So where did all the people go?" Lila mused.

Dr. Cooper only shook his head. "They've fled, I would guess. They've evacuated the island, and very suddenly. I'll wager that our Mr. MacKenzie and his people now have this island all to themselves."

Jay recalled MacKenzie's note. " '. . . come quickly, the island is . . .' Just what did he really mean by that?"

"We're going back," said Dr. Cooper.

The return was much quicker in the daylight. They had one objective in mind: that strange, forbidden trail MacKenzie would not let them explore, the trail where Dulaney met his tragic death.

Within sight of the village, they ducked behind some rocks. They could see right down the main street, which had many people going about their daily business. Somehow the Coopers had to get to that trail without being seen.

"Lila, you be the eyes," Dr. Cooper whispered.

She concealed herself in the crook of an old tree and watched the village street. Every once in a while, but only for a few seconds, the street would be empty.

One such moment came. She waved her hand, and Jay dashed down the road into the village, behind a woodshed, and then, with a sharp cut sideways, down that forbidden trail and out of sight just as some carpenters reappeared in the street. They were armed and seemed a bit edgy.

Dr. Cooper did the spying next, and Lila was the one to make a dash for the trail. With only seconds to spare, she reached it and slipped unnoticed into the jungle.

Dr. Cooper waited for his moment, and followed. Finally they were reassembled and hurrying along.

"All right," Dr. Cooper whispered, "here's the fork we came to last night. No splitting up this time . . ."

"Thank you," said Lila.

"We'll just take the left fork and see what we find."

They slipped through the jungle, ducking under

those wet, hanging vines, darting this way and that around stumps, fallen logs, and bogs, watching and listening.

Jay pointed up at a tall tree with a large bird's nest in the branches, empty. Along the way they noticed several more, as well as empty burrows here and there. Dulaney was right again. The animals had fled.

Before long they glimpsed the light of a clearing through the trees. They crouched down to remain concealed, slinking along close to the wet, mossy ground until they could reach the clearing's edge. Then they fanned out, finding concealment behind a large rock, a tree, and a large bush.

There was something wrong, something creepy about this place. The tall trees overhung it as if they were weeping, or half dead, and a strange, unpleasant stench pervaded the air like something dead and rotting. The place was silent, and the ground was rocky. The many huge stones set up on end here and there made it look like a primitive temple or shrine. They could have been astrological markers, or tables, or pedestals, or. . . .

"Altars?" Dr. Cooper mused.

In the center of the clearing was a very wide dip in the ground, or a hole. They could not see its bottom, only the edge. Perhaps it was some kind of fire pit. Dr. Cooper cautiously ventured into the clearing, followed by his son and daughter. As they neared the center, they could see the sides of the supposed fire pit dropping further and further down, and it was only when the Coopers finally stood right at the edge that they could see a sandy bottom about fifteen feet below.

The floor of the pit was littered with dry, sunbleached bones.

"Lord God," Dr. Cooper muttered in a very troubled prayer, "now what?"

"A sacrificial pit?" asked Jay, as if it even had to be asked.

Dr. Cooper knelt down for a closer look. "So . . . there's some paganism and witchcraft being practiced here. The pit has been used recently. . ." he observed, and that very observation was making him ill. "One of the animal carcasses hasn't been there too long."

"Dad," Jay said very weakly. "I think I see some *human* bones down there!"

Dr. Cooper analyzed the pit itself. "Another volcanic vent, I think. It could penetrate deep into the island. Some kind of carnivorous animal must live down there . . . something that feeds on the . . . on the offerings."

He stood up and walked away from the pit. What was the point in talking about it anymore?

"Do you suppose this is what we may have heard last night?" Jay asked. "Some kind of ceremony going on here?"

"I don't know," said Dr. Cooper, and he was deep in thought. "I really don't think the voices we heard last night came from this direction." He looked across the clearing and into the jungle further on. "I think they could have come from over there somewhere, which means that we may not have seen all there is to see."

"I've seen all *I* want to see," said Lila.

"I'm going to confront MacKenzie about this. In the meantime, I'd like to check that trail over there and see—"

A twig snapped. There was a rustling in the jungle. The Coopers dove for the trail by which they had come.

But now it was guarded by armed men, their rifles ready and aiming.

FIVE

More guards appeared at another entrance to the clearing, and they too brandished their weapons. The Coopers were trapped.

"Dr. Cooper," called a voice, "you should know better! This island is full of eyes, and I know everything they see."

Of course. There stood Adam MacKenzie, between two bodyguards, looking at the Coopers with shock and anger all over his face.

Dr. Cooper was getting a little tired of all this mystery and all these guns. He stepped forward boldly and stood face to face with this strange island ruler.

"Is this why you didn't want us venturing into the jungle? Just what is this place, and what goes on here?"

But MacKenzie could not respond. His face had gone pale, and his eyes widened with horror.

"Protectors!" he shouted.

Every armed man immediately dug out his red scarf and wrapped it around his neck. Every face was etched with fear. Some of the guns shook in trembling hands.

"Mor—Moro-Kunda!" MacKenzie cried with a trembling voice. "Do *not* move, you three, or I will have my men open fire on you right here!"

53

The Coopers looked at all the trembling men, and something horrible began to dawn on them.

"Dad, he's trying to set us up," Jay whispered desperately.

"I know," Dr. Cooper replied. He spoke to Mac-Kenzie. "Listen to me, MacKenzie, and listen well. I don't know what this Moro-Kunda of yours is, but I assure you, you are now tampering with a God who is more than a match for any curses or powers you can dream up."

"I'm very sorry, Doctor," said MacKenzie. "Believe me, I mean you no harm. But you have invaded sacred ground here, and now there is no question that all three of you have contracted the curse yourselves."

"It won't work, MacKenzie," Dr. Cooper said very coldly.

But MacKenzie only shook his head sorrowfully. "You have tampered with the secret powers of the island. Yes, Dr. Cooper, this is why I warned you not to venture into the jungle. You should have listened. Now it may be too late!"

MacKenzie nodded and the guards moved in, grabbing all three of them, taking away their packs and Dr. Cooper's gun.

"You give me no choice," said MacKenzie with a glint in his eye. "For the sake of my people here, I must have you confined until the curse has . . . finished its work."

The confinement hut was built solidly, with thick log walls and a heavy plank door (locked of course). The windows were mere peepholes and the tiny room was illuminated by one light bulb hanging from the ceiling. A guard stood outside.

Jay and Lila sat on two cots. Dr. Cooper walked

aimlessly up and down the floor, thinking, praying, thinking.

"I believe," said Jay, "I'm getting scared."

"So you finally admit it," said Lila.

"Enough, you two!" Dr. Cooper snapped. "Fear is understandable enough, but surrendering to it will never get us out of here."

"But all I can think about is Mr. Dulaney's face, and his eyes . . ." Lila said, and then she whispered, "Dad, is that going to happen to us?"

Dr. Cooper stared at the thatched roof above them as he said, "Psalm 91 is good for times like this, especially the parts about the Lord delivering us from the snare of the trapper, and from the pestilence that stalks in the darkness."

Jay brightened a little as he let the psalm roll through his mind. " '. . . no evil will befall you, nor will any plague come near your tent,' " he quoted.

"Or near our confinement hut!" said Lila, a little more encouraged.

Dr. Cooper kept walking up and down, thinking and then speaking. "So what I'm doing now is praying that the Lord will reveal to me just how we might get ourselves out of this mess."

"What about the curse, Dad?" Jay asked. "What about this Moro-Kunda? It *has* killed two men—you said that yourself. MacKenzie's not bluffing."

"No, son, he isn't," Dr. Cooper admitted. "But the question is, is this truly a demonic work, or is it some clever trick MacKenzie uses to scare people? Think about it. I'm sure he has the whole village waiting now to see what's going to happen to us, and if something does happen . . ."

"He'll have all those people eating out of his hand!" said Lila.

"Exactly. This—this curse just seems a little too

handy, a little too much under his control to dish out whenever he wants, on whomever he wants."

"So how do we keep from ending up like Tommy and Dulaney?"

"We anticipate," said Dr. Cooper. "We plan for any eventuality."

"What if it's demonic?" said Jay.

"We pray beforehand so we can rebuke it and chase it off."

"And if it's a disease?" asked Lila.

"We pray for God's protection and healing mercy."

"So what else could it be?" Jay wondered.

Dr. Cooper kept looking up at the roof, and then at the walls.

"I don't know," he said, "I guess we'll just have to find out when it—uh—gets here."

Hours passed, and the angle of the sun beaming through those small peepholes became more and more shallow until the sun dipped below the trees and finally set beyond the Pacific horizon.

The Coopers were given nothing to eat, for no one was allowed to approach the hut. Occasionally they could hear a conversation outside, always in hushed tones.

"How are they?" someone would ask.

"Still alive, and quiet," the guard would answer.

Then there would be very hushed discussions about how long "it" would take, and how these foolish visitors should have known better, and how the great leader was always so wise and so right about such things.

"It's like a cross between death row and the zoo," Jay said bitterly.

"Sounds like their great leader is making quite a show of it," said Dr. Cooper.

"I just don't want to die," Lila kept saying to herself.

The sunlight through the little peepholes finally ebbed away completely, and it was night. The village outside grew quiet. The guards changed. A few more hours passed.

"How are you feeling?" Dr. Cooper asked.

"Bored, that's all," said Lila.

"I almost fell asleep," said Jay. "I don't know if—hey!"

"Oh-oh," said Lila.

Dr. Cooper braced himself against the log wall. The light bulb hanging from the ceiling began to sway back and forth, making the shadows all around the room stretch and sway like dark, taunting ghosts. Beneath them, the earth stirred with a very low rumble.

"Earthquake," said Dr. Cooper.

They could hear the guard outside muttering to himself in frightened tones, "M-moro-Kunda!"

Someone else added, "Just as we were told! It's beginning!"

The light bulb swung crazily from its wire as the shadows in the room went berserk. Then, with one final swing, it slapped against a ceiling rafter and popped with a fiery flash. The room went totally black.

"Oh, great!" said Jay.

The rumbling and shaking continued for just a few more seconds, and then subsided.

The Coopers stood perfectly still in the blackness, as if waiting for something else to happen. Nothing did. They relaxed.

"Dulaney was no madman," said Dr. Cooper. "He was right about the tides, right about the animals, and now we see he was right about the earthquakes."

" '. . . the island is' . . . in big trouble!" said Jay, completing MacKenzie's note.

"Now what?" asked Lila.

"Lila," said Dr. Cooper, "you pray first. We'll all take turns."

And so they prayed, sitting there in that tight little hut, in the dark, waiting for whatever it was to come for them. Lila poured her heart out to God; Jay prayed with great fervor and just a little anger; Dr. Cooper prayed mostly for his children, that both of them could remain alive to serve the Lord for many more years to come. Soon the Coopers were alert and poised, ready for the worst, and yet their hearts were at rest. God was with them, and that was all they needed to know.

Late into the night, a familiar, eerie sound found its way through those small peepholes into the dark room.

"They're at it again," said Dr. Cooper.

Yes. There were those wailings again, and those strange chants, and the eerie cheering.

"The same as last night," said Lila, and then she added with a chilling tone, "the night Mr. Dulaney died."

"What do you think, Dad?" asked Jay. "Could they be trying to invoke the curse on us right now?"

"It wouldn't surprise me," Dr. Cooper answered, going to one of the peepholes.

A very dim light shone through that peephole and projected a small square of light on Dr. Cooper's face as he peered out into the jungle. His eyes were intense and watchful.

"You see something?" Jay asked.

"Candle," he answered.

Jay and Lila went to the peephole to take turns looking. Far away, like some distant, twinkling star, the light from that torch moved steadily through the jungle, meandering, pausing, lurking.

"What is he doing out there?" Lila was dying to know.

Suddenly she felt Dr. Cooper's grip on her shoulder. She froze. He was listening for something. All three stood there silently, and waited.

Footsteps in the grass outside? Perhaps it was the wind. Was the guard making that noise? They thought they heard a scratching, a rustling of fibers, and a very slow, very steady crumbling like the crushing of dry leaves.

Dr. Cooper's eyes, still illuminated by that little beam of light, turned toward the ceiling, but it was too dark to see anything.

But as they listened, and tilted their heads this way and that . . . yes, the sound was above them. It was so very quiet! It could have been a mouse, or a spider, or a falling leaf.

Silence. Had the maker of the sound gone away?

Then came a new noise. It was high-pitched, wavering, humming, almost like the sound of a distant airplane. They first heard it somewhere in the thatched ceiling over their heads, but it came closer, lower, and began to move around the room.

Dr. Cooper's eyes vanished from the little square of light.

Zzzzzzzzzzz . . . zzzzzzzzzz. . . .

Suddenly there was the scratch and flare of a lighting match. The yellow light filled the room. Dr. Cooper held the match high. His eyes darted around.

Then they widened.

"Get down!" he shouted.

Jay and Lila hit the floor. The match went out. Blackness returned.

Zzzzzzzzzzz . . . zzzzzzzzzz. . . . The sound was sinking lower, coming closer.

Another match lit up the room. It shook, it streaked about the hut. Dr. Cooper was dashing here and there, ducking, dodging, his eyes wild with excitement.

"Do you see it?" he cried. "Do you see it?"

SIX

Jay and Lila looked here and there, spinning every direction, trying to see what their father was yelling about.

What was that? It was only a blur in the dim light, a fuzzy blotch meandering about in the air, swerving this way and that. Suddenly, like a tiny missile, it shot towards Jay.

"Duck!" Dr. Cooper yelled.

Jay had already ducked as the thing shot by his ear with a loud ZZZZZZZZZZZING like a revved engine. Jay and Lila leaped to their feet, looking to see where it went.

The match went out.

"Dad!" Jay yelled.

"Don't let it land on you!" was all he could say as he struggled with another match.

ZZZZZZZZING! The sound went by Lila this time, and she dove and tumbled in the dark over a cot.

"Cover your heads!" Dr. Cooper yelled.

They pulled their jacket collars up around their faces as Dr. Cooper finally got another match lit.

ZZZZZZZING! went the dark spot in the air, zipping right toward Dr. Cooper. He ducked, and the thing bumped into the wall. Its whirring stopped for just a second, and there was a tiny puff of vapor.

ZZZZZZZ . . . It continued flying about the room,

buzzing at them, diving, chasing, getting more aggressive with each attempt.

It zzzzzinged over Lila's head, but she ducked. Jay took a swat at it with a blanket. ZZZZING! It came at him, and he leaped aside.

Then the match went out again, and Lila screamed, "It's on me! It's on me!"

Jay snatched the blanket and thrashed in the dark at Lila's body. He could hear that ZZZZZZZZ somewhere on her back.

Another match lit.

"Get that coat off!" Dr. Cooper yelled.

Lila ripped the coat off and threw it to the floor. The sound broke loose from the coat and continued flying around the room.

ZZZZZING! Jay ducked again, then swatted against the wall with the blanket. The whirring sputtered and started again.

Dr. Cooper leaped onto a cot and went after the thing with his hat, swatting, ducking, swatting again.

The air was filling with a very strong, burning odor. ZZZZZ . . . zzzzzz . . . ZZZZZZZ went the thing.

The match went out. Dr. Cooper was struggling, stumbling in the dark. Suddenly there was a loud, metallic clang.

Dr. Cooper let out a bloodcurdling scream.

"Dad!" Jay and Lila shouted into the blackness.

The lock on the door rattled. The bolt was thrown aside. The door swung open and a big, burly silhouette appeared in the doorway, shining a light about the room.

From somewhere in the dark, a knee came up in the guard's face, and then BONG! A large metal pot struck the guard's head. The big man sank to the floor.

Jay and Lila were speechless and terrified. What had happened?

The guard's flashlight was grabbed up from his limp hand.

"Don't move, you two," came Dr. Cooper's voice.

"Dad, are you all right?" Jay cried out.

"Yes, thank the Lord," he said. "Don't move!"

The beam of the flashlight swept about the room in search of something, finally coming to rest in the middle of the floor.

"Ah, there it is," said Dr. Cooper.

Jay and Lila saw a bizarre sight: a dark, smoldering circle was slowly spreading out over the floorboard, sending up a strong, burning odor.

In the center of that dark, smoldering circle was . . . The Thing.

"What is *that*?" Lila asked in horror.

Dr. Cooper shook his head in wonderment and replied, "Moro-Kunda."

"A *bug*?" Jay asked in unbelief.

"A cleft-winged African tiger fly," Dr. Cooper replied, kneeling down and probing the huge insect with a twig. "I've never really seen one—until now. Lila, we'll have to discard your coat."

They looked at Lila's coat, tossed on the floor, and it too had a dark, burning spot on it, slowly growing and sending up a wisp of smoke.

"What is it?" she asked. "Acid?"

"Yes, the insect's venom. Look here."

Dr. Cooper raised the insect just a little with the stick and pointed out a vicious-looking stinger that seemed to be dripping boiling water. Every drop sent up a cloud of putrid, burning vapor. "Very acidic, and very deadly. The stinger hardly leaves a mark, but the venom works into the bloodstream immediately and causes the symptoms observed on Tommy and then on Dulaney. Both of them were burned, consumed, from the inside out."

It was only now that Jay started getting the shakes. He sat down on a cot and tried to get a grip on himself.

Lila had to know, "But what on earth happened? We heard you scream."

"Was it convincing?" Dr. Cooper asked.

"Oh, brother!" said Jay.

"Well . . ." Dr. Cooper said with a smile, "I knew I'd finally hit the tiger fly squarely with that old pan over there." He looked over to the corner of the room, and Jay and Lila saw a very large metal pot lying on the floor next to the fallen guard. "I think that was supposed to be our toilet," Dr. Cooper added with a twinkle in his eye.

"Wooo . . ." said Lila. "I'm glad we haven't had anything to drink."

"Anyway, I figured I might take advantage of our situation and give the guard what he'd been waiting for. It was a gamble, but when he heard me scream, he must have thought that the curse had struck, and he couldn't wait to get in here and see what had happened."

"And you clanged him!" said Jay triumphantly.

"And now the Lord has helped us do something Adam MacKenzie wasn't counting on: we've lived to expose his little trick."

"Ahhhhh . . ." said Jay.

"You mean, MacKenzie planted that bug in our hut to kill us?" Lila asked.

Dr. Cooper shined the flashlight toward the ceiling. "It would have been easy to insert the fly through that thatched roof. That must have been the sound we heard. As for the fly itself, it isn't even native to the South Seas. Someone—and we can all guess who—imported them just for this purpose, I would say. It would make for a very convincing 'curse.'"

"That it would," said Lila, very impressed.

"Anyone for getting out of here?"

They locked the guard inside the hut, using his own keys.

"Now what?" asked Jay.

"We need to get our belongings back, and—" Dr. Cooper stopped in midsentence. He was looking toward the jungle.

Jay and Lila looked, and there was that little point of light again.

"And I would like to find out just what that character is up to," Dr. Cooper said.

They slipped silently into the jungle, crouching under the wet, gooey vines again, moving along that same trail with that one flashlight taken from the guard, now in Dr. Cooper's hand.

They were closing in on that point of light. Another branch in the trail seemed to lead straight toward it.

When near enough to discern the flicker of the torch's flame, they moved very slowly, very silently.

Candle didn't seem to be going anywhere now. Evidently he was standing still in one spot.

Dr. Cooper turned off the flashlight, and they moved closer in the inky darkness, placing their fingers in the soft, wet ground to find the trail.

The flame of the torch was very close now, only about twenty feet away.

Dr. Cooper raised his head just enough to peer over the bushes at that flame. He looked for a moment . . . and then let out a sigh and his body relaxed as if deflating just a little. He had a very curious expression on his face.

Jay and Lila rose up to take a look.

That torch wasn't sitting on top of Candle's head where it usually was; it sat, all by itself, on a large rock.

The Coopers came out of hiding and went to the

rock for a closer inspection. There was nothing unusual about the torch or the rock, but finding the two together in the middle of the night was certainly a puzzle.

"Is this . . . well, is this some kind of ruse?" Jay wondered. "I get the feeling we've been tricked."

"It doesn't make a bit of sense, does it?" said Dr. Cooper. "But let's think about it for a moment: he managed to trick us into thinking he was here. Is he trying to trick anyone else into thinking the same?"

"So where is he really?" Lila inquired.

"And why is he there, and why doesn't he want anyone to know it?" asked Jay.

Dr. Cooper couldn't help laughing a little, maybe out of frustration. "Well, so far this whole trip has been very consistent: questions, questions, and more questions, but no answers."

"And that party is still going on," said Jay, nodding his head toward the many voices still wailing and singing somewhere out in the jungle.

"We'll drop by for a visit," said Dr. Cooper.

Their hearts were pounding as they pushed on through the jungle, following the winding trail, always taking quick little moments to listen and watch. The sounds of wailing and chanting grew closer. The Coopers kept moving.

Then Dr. Cooper stopped and pointed at his nose. Jay and Lila sniffed the air. They could smell something burning, like the smell of sparks or hot stones. They pressed on, step by step, picking up that smell more and more.

Now they could see what looked like another clearing coming up, and an orange, fiery glow shining on the trees. The villagers must be having some kind of bonfire.

The "party" was in full swing when the Coopers

finally slinked and prowled up to the clearing's edge. Lila found a good spot in a tree from which to watch, Jay climbed up on a very handy boulder, and Dr. Cooper was tall enough simply to conceal himself and observe what was happening in the clearing.

The area looked like a large, outdoor amphitheater, with logs rolled into place to serve as benches, all facing a huge fire pit in the center, now red, glowing, and covered over with stones. The benches were full of villagers—mothers, fathers, children, workers—and all of them were wailing and moaning some strange chant as if in a devilish, hypnotic worship service. The participants were entranced, and swayed back and forth like a field of grass, their eyes vacant and staring, their necks craned as if they were hanging by their hair.

But it was that glowing, smoldering, fiery mound of stones that grabbed the Coopers' attention. With great amazement and dread, they watched as former college professors, lawyers, and executives, like puppets possessed, stepped barefoot onto the hot, glowing rocks, walked over them, and then stepped off onto the ground again to the cheers of the crowd, their feet unaffected by the incredible, searing heat.

Having passed through this fiery test, they then knelt before Adam MacKenzie, who stood at the other end of the mound, officiating over the whole ritual, encouraging the new initiates, and basking in the admiration and glory.

Jay had seen pictures and films of such bizarre rituals. "Firewalking!" he exclaimed in a whisper.

Dr. Cooper nodded. "Now I recall something about the dead man Tommy: the hair on his feet was singed, and there was ash dust under his toenails. *He* was a firewalker."

The Coopers remained very still in the darkness, spellbound by the bizarre ritual. Now some women went up to the mound and looked across it at MacKenzie, praying for his blessing. He stretched his hand toward them and beckoned to them to come. In a trancelike stupor, they took a step, then another, one bare foot at a time, the fire-reddened smoke billowing and creeping around their feet.

Dr. Cooper was angry and ashamed at what he was seeing.

"A firewalking party!" he said, shaking his head. "People under demonic power, walking on incredibly hot stones without being burned, and they think they'll find salvation in *that!*"

"Some beautiful new world," said Jay.

"It's nothing but tragic! They've obviously turned away from God and from the truth of Jesus Christ, and now, thinking they've discovered some great new cosmic power, they've done nothing but fall into the darkness and bondage of witchcraft and paganism! Civilized, Western, supposedly Christian intellectuals . . . firewalking!" Dr. Cooper shook his head again.

"What was that Scripture?" Lila asked. "Something about turning away from the truth."

" '. . . and following deceitful spirits and doctrines of demons,' " Dr. Cooper replied. "First Timothy, chapter four, I think. Satan has made fools of these people!"

"Well," said Jay, "I can see old MacKenzie sure has! He has them thinking *he's* God!"

"But now we know where he and all his followers are." Dr. Cooper gestured to Jay and Lila, and they came down from their observation perches. "While the cat's away, these mice are going to play. Let's have a look in his cottage."

Except for two or three watchmen making their rounds here and there, the village was deserted while all its inhabitants were "discussing spiritual matters."

MacKenzie's cottage stood on the edge of the village, surrounded on three sides by the jungle. There was plenty of cover, and the Coopers found plenty of places to hide. They went around to the side of the house away from the village square and climbed a tree to reach the veranda. One by one, they stepped over the veranda's railing and ducked into the dark shadows at the rear of the cottage.

Dr. Cooper inched along toward a back door and tried it. It was unlocked. MacKenzie was apparently a very confident man. Dr. Cooper swung the door open, and they slipped inside.

The cottage was well furnished; MacKenzie was obviously well-to-do here in his little island kingdom. The living room contained souvenirs from all over the South Seas, from primitive weapons to pagan animal amulets, charms of stone, and trinkets of bone. There were idols everywhere, images of monsters, snakes, and lizards, staring in all directions from the floor, walls, and ceiling with fiery, jeweled eyes, hideous faces, and gruesome, bare-teethed expressions. The place looked like a demonic hall of fame.

Along one wall was a vast library containing hundreds of books. Jay looked over some of the titles and found that most of them dealt with mysticism, witchcraft, sorcery, fortunetelling, and on and on.

"Is there a Bible anywhere in all that mess?" Dr. Cooper asked.

"I don't see one," Jay replied.

"Well, what did we expect?" said Lila.

"But isn't it strange," mused Dr. Cooper, "that a man who'd spent so many years on the field as a very committed and trustworthy missionary would stray so thoroughly into paganism, leaving behind even his trust in the Word of God? I find that so hard to accept."

Dr. Cooper noticed another door leading out of the main living room, and pushed it open. The beam of the flashlight revealed what looked like an office. There were more bookshelves, some files, some blueprints, and a very large desk.

"We might find something in here, so—"

ZZZzzzzzz!

Dr. Cooper leaped back and quickly closed the door.

"Dad?" Jay asked. "What's the matter? What is it?"

Dr. Cooper exhaled very slowly and calmed himself.

"Once in one night is more than enough!" he said.

He cracked the door again and let the beam of the flashlight move around the room inside, from floor to filing cabinet to bookshelves, and then to a cupboard with the door slightly ajar.

ZZZZZZZZZZ! Even Jay and Lila could hear it from the living room, and they immediately ducked, crouched, got ready to run, got ready to fight, got ready, period!

"Well . . ." said Dr. Cooper. "Let's have a look at this."

He eased slowly into the room. His beam was certainly upsetting something inside that cupboard. Jay and Lila stood just outside, peeking through the doorway as Dr. Cooper approached the cupboard and reached for the cupboard door.

"Dad—" Lila couldn't help saying, her hand over her mouth.

Dr. Cooper motioned for silence and then, very slowly, very carefully, began to pull the door open.

He opened it just a few inches. Yes, the very familiar sound was coming from inside. He used the flashlight to get a better look.

Jay and Lila stayed right where they were, watching wide-eyed.

Then Dr. Cooper slowly opened the door the rest of the way.

"It's all right," he said finally. "They're caged."

Jay and Lila tiptoed in to look, and were sickened at the sight. There, on the bottom shelf of Adam MacKenzie's office cupboard, in a very tightly-meshed cage, were dozens, a virtual swarm of deadly tiger flies.

"Quite a collection," said Dr. Cooper.

"Moro-Kunda . . . in a cage," exclaimed Jay.

Dr. Cooper was more than ready to close that door again, muffling the angry, whirring sound. "This confirms our suspicions. I'm afraid we have a ruthless killer on our hands, a deceiver of the most heinous kind."

Dr. Cooper went to the desk and checked through the drawers. "He has my gun somewhere, and I'd like it back."

There was no gun in the desk, but Dr. Cooper did find a manila folder that intrigued him. Inside the folder were blueprints, some letters, and some photographs.

"Well," he said, quickly going through it all, "what do you know! Blueprints for a church . . . letters from MacKenzie . . . and a picture of . . . Well, of course!"

Jay and Lila had only begun searching through some other cabinets when suddenly—footsteps! Footsteps out in the square! Many of them, all hurrying, running!

"Let's move," said Dr. Cooper, and they darted to the office door.

Too late! People were everywhere, and by the way they scurried about, looking here and there, barking commands and answers to each other, it was obvious that something had gone quite wrong.

"I think they're on to us," said Jay.

"Keep calm," Dr. Cooper said. "Don't move."

"What are we going to do?" Jay asked.

"Look!" whispered Lila. "There's MacKenzie!"

He was hurrying across the square and right toward the cottage, eight armed men with him including the guard from the confinement hut.

Jay spoke for all three: "We're trapped!"

SEVEN

"Oh, where's your gun?" Lila wished she could know.

But Dr. Cooper was not beside Jay anymore. He had gone back into MacKenzie's office.

"Dad!" Lila hissed. "What are you doing?"

"Get behind me," he said.

Adam MacKenzie bounded up the front steps like an attacking general, his henchmen right behind him. From the look on his face and the gait of his walk, it was obvious he smelled trouble.

"Check every room!" he ordered, and his men began to scatter throughout the cottage.

But Dr. Cooper saved them the trouble. He stepped out of MacKenzie's office and said, "We're right here, everybody."

The men immediately made a move for Dr. Cooper, but were stopped abruptly by a terrified order from MacKenzie. "Hold it! Don't touch him! Get back, get back!"

They got back and they got back fast, all their eyes glued on what Dr. Cooper now held in his hands.

"Easy . . ." said MacKenzie, with a pale face and a shaking voice, backing up against the wall. "Just . . . just take it easy . . ."

Dr. Cooper was holding the cage containing the swarm of very angry tiger flies. The cage was now inverted, the lid unlatched and ready to drop open if Dr. Cooper so much as moved his hand from it.

"Tell them to drop their guns," said Dr. Cooper.

"Do it," said MacKenzie. Three rifles and five revolvers clunked to the floor.

The tiger flies whirred, buzzed, plinked, and thumped against the walls of the cage. They did not like being disturbed.

MacKenzie kept gazing at Dr. Cooper, Dr. Cooper kept his eyes on MacKenzie, and every other eye was on that one hand that held that lid shut.

"Dr. Cooper," MacKenzie finally said, "you are indeed a formidable man, and very hard to be rid of."

Dr. Cooper glanced at the guard from the confinement hut as he asked MacKenzie, "I suppose he told you about our little encounter?"

"He will be punished. I gave him a clear order not to enter the hut for any reason."

"Or he would have seen . . . one of these."

"What are they?" the guard asked.

"Suppose I tell him?" Dr. Cooper asked MacKenzie.

MacKenzie looked at his men, then at Dr. Cooper, and sighed a nervous sigh. "I do concede, Doctor, that you have the upper hand at the moment. But I'm a reasonable man, as I'm sure you are. I'm ready to negotiate. What is it you want?"

"You still have our belongings."

"John," MacKenzie said to one of his men, "bring their backpacks and anything else that belongs to them."

John hurried out of the room.

Dr. Cooper's eyes were alert and full of cunning as he said, "We're getting out of here, MacKenzie—or whoever you are. We've had quite enough of you and this insane, demonized island. We're going back to our boat and we're sailing immediately. Agreed?"

MacKenzie's men looked very uneasy, but MacKenzie broke the strained silence by answering, "That's . . . that's reasonable, Doctor. I think it's . . . well . . . it's what we both want anyway, isn't it?"

The man named John reappeared, carrying the Coopers' backpacks and the 357.

"Check the gun, Jay," said Dr. Cooper.

Jay picked it up, checked it for ammunition and action, and then helped his father buckle it on. The three of them quickly grabbed up their packs and then, with Dr. Cooper still holding that cage for all to see, went out the front door.

There were shouts and stares from many upset villagers when the Coopers stepped out onto the veranda, but MacKenzie appeared in his doorway very quickly and called, "Be still, everyone! Let them pass. They are not to be hampered in any way."

"Thank you, sir," said Dr. Cooper. "I wouldn't want a killer plague unleashed on my island either."

From all around the square, MacKenzie's people, the old, the young, the Europeans, the Americans, the Polynesians, watched as the three mysterious visitors moved stealthily, back to back, across the square. Some were whispering about what it was Dr. Cooper held in his hands.

MacKenzie answered several whispered questions by saying simply, "It's a bomb."

Some whispered about the curse of Moro-Kunda, and others commented on how these three accursed victims were still alive and how strange that was.

The Coopers made their way up the street, followed at a distance by what was beginning to look like a very curious and very dangerous mob. Obviously, the Coopers would never be invited back here.

They reached the trail that led into the jungle and back to the cove.

"Let's move," said Dr. Cooper, and they broke into a run, dashing this way and that, following that winding trail through the thick jungle. Jay and Lila kept the beams of their flashlights on the ground so Dr. Cooper could see his way, considering his deadly cargo. The tangled vines and tendrils reached down out of the dark, slapping, whipping, dripping on them.

Lila had not forgotten the bridge. As they ran closer to it, she prayed for courage and determination just to get across that thing and not be afraid. Perhaps the darkness would make it easier.

Now they could hear the roar of the water in that very deep chasm. Then they came into the open on the brink of those sheer cliffs, and there was that awful bridge!

Dr. Cooper came to a halt and secured the little latch on the lid to the cage. He had a particular destination in mind for these foul insects, and he wanted them all to get there together.

He looked down at Lila and gave her a loving squeeze. "Can you make it?"

"I . . . I *have* to, that's all," she said.

Lila was praying as she stepped onto the first half-rotted board and grabbed the rope rails.

The cold air chilled her with the mist of the foaming, swirling water far below, and the roar seemed even louder now in the darkness. Lila tried not to hear it and concentrated on where she put her feet. She stepped on the next board, and it sagged a bit under her weight, letting out a disturbing creak. The board after that was missing altogether; there was nothing beneath her but cold, dark space. She stepped over it with a quick prayer. She knew that monster was down there growling, spinning, ready to swallow her in an instant. The bridge began to sink and then rise, stretch and then pull, heave up and then down, and Lila could feel her stomach turning in a hundred directions.

But she was making it! *Oh, help me, Jesus!*

Dr. Cooper touched Jay. "Go ahead, son. I have to see to these bugs."

Jay stepped out onto the dizzying bridge, and started carefully step-by-stepping his way across.

"Hurry!" Dr. Cooper shouted to both of them, and they hurried.

Lila was just reaching the other side of the bridge when suddenly she screamed, "Dad!"

Jay was almost across. Dr. Cooper ran onto the bridge.

"What is it?" he shouted.

Now Jay hollered, "Dad, it's the boat!"

Lila stood on the other side, looking down with horror toward the cove. "It's on fire!"

Dr. Cooper stepped cautiously but quickly from crumbling board to crumbling board, straining to see what his children were seeing. The bridge reeled like a cracked whip under his feet, and he had to hang on with only one hand so as not to drop that deadly cage. Jay, just ahead, craned his neck for a better view.

"Dad," he shouted, "they're burning the boat!"

"The fools!" Dr. Cooper said. "Those explosives on board will detonate for sure, and destroy that entire harbor."

Jay's face turned pale. Yes, that was right! There were enough plastic explosives in the hold to make a crater of the entire cove.

Dr. Cooper wanted desperately to be rid of that horrible cage. Oh, to have both hands free again and get off this bridge! He tried to get his bearings from what he could see of the rocky cliffs on either side of the chasm. Was he directly over that whirlpool yet?

What? The rope rail on the left snapped and dropped like a broken kite string! The bridge twisted crazily, the world spun upside down, sideways, back again, rocking this way and that, a hat went sailing, fluttering, meandering down into the black nothing. Jake Cooper's legs and arms kicked and hooked on to a tangle of ropes and boards. He was upside down. His blood pounded in his head. With nothing but the darkness of that chasm all around, he kept swinging, rocking, swaying, like a fly in a web, like a fish in a net.

ZZZZZZZZZZ!

The cage had snagged on a shred of rope, and now it was dangling, the lid cracked open—right next to his head! He could see the angry insects buzzing against the wire mesh sides, he could see their licking red tongues and dripping stingers.

He could hear Lila screaming. But now where was Jay? He twisted his head slowly away from the cage and looked ahead.

Oh no! Jay was hanging from twisted, tangled shreds of rope, trying desperately to crawl hand-over-hand to the side of the cliff. Boards were dropping like rotted teeth on either side of him. His pack was pulling him down.

Sounds! Lights! On the far side of the chasm stood several of MacKenzie's men.

"Dad!" Lila screamed from somewhere.

ZZZZZZZZZ! whined the angry black insects, some of them trying to squeeze out through the slightly open lid.

There was nothing to grab, no way to get free. Dr. Cooper groped about with one hand, trying to find any other rope, anything he could use to lift himself back up again. He could feel his legs and other arm losing their grip, sliding slowly out of that tangled web. His head was hanging down toward that horrible, roaring throat of raging water. The tiger flies were buzzing in his ear.

"Dad!" Lila screamed again, and then her scream became a constricted gurgle as if she were choking.

"Lila!" he shouted. "What's happening?"

"Let go of her!" Jay hollered.

"Doctor Cooper!" came a loathsome, terribly familiar, snickering voice. MacKenzie! Dr. Cooper twisted his head toward the rocky cliff behind him.

Yes, there stood the madman with several of his henchmen, and there was a knife in his hand. *He* had cut the rope!

"Your daughter is in good hands, I assure you!" said MacKenzie, looking across the chasm to the other side.

Dr. Cooper looked that way, and . . . Oh, Lord God, no! Now he could see her. She was being held by a huge thug, and even though she was struggling, he kept his big arms clamped around her.

Dr. Cooper could feel a terrible rage mixed with a terrible fear as he shouted, "Let her go!"

ZZZZZZZ! said the flies in response, bouncing and clinking about in the cage. Legs and tongues were exploring that crack.

"Speak softly, Dr. Cooper," said MacKenzie. "My little pets there have very sensitive ears, you know."

No! One had gotten out. It was now crawling with its well-coordinated, spindly, pipe-cleaner legs down the same rope Dr. Cooper hung from.

Slowly. Slowly. Free your hand, Jake Cooper! There.

MacKenzie kept talking. "I wouldn't worry too much about your fair daughter, Dr. Cooper. I assure you, I'll take good care of her. She'll be very useful to me."

Wham! Dr. Cooper found a piece of board and quickly crushed the insect. A wisp of vapor wafted from the rope where it had been. The venom began to dissolve the rope. *Come on, Jake, find something else to grab!*

"Let her go, you creep!" shouted Jay again, hanging from the frayed ropes by two arms and one leg.

MacKenzie only laughed and said, "If I were you, Jay Cooper, I would be worrying about myself!"

Ping! The rope snapped, and Dr. Cooper dropped. His hand found another frayed shred just in time. He jerked to a stop, his body swinging crazily, his legs dangling over that black, infinite space.

MacKenzie couldn't help laughing at him. "I see that now your precious cageful has become your enemy, and I now have your daughter in my possession. Looks like I have the advantage again, doesn't it?" MacKenzie looked across to the other side of the chasm, and his eyes brightened. "Ah, I see my men have returned."

The man holding Lila was now joined by three others, and each of them carried a large, brightly burning torch.

MacKenzie explained. "You see, Doctor, you were supposed to be dead by now, and therefore I thought it best to have my men burn your boat. You would no longer be needing it, and . . . well, now there will be no way for outsiders to know you've ever been here."

Dr. Cooper had to tell him. "MacKenzie, listen. There are powerful explosives aboard that boat! Please be sure all your men are a safe distance away. It could explode any moment."

MacKenzie looked at his torch-bearing henchmen, and they all looked down toward the cove and shrugged with mocking smiles on their faces. There certainly had been no explosion.

"Good Doctor, I thought Christians didn't lie!" Then MacKenzie smiled a cold, calculating smile and said, "Oh well. We all do what we have to do, don't we,

Doctor? You understand, I must protect the sanctity of this place, especially from inquisitive snoops like you. You are a very hard man to be rid of, Doctor, but as they say, if at first you don't succeed . . ." MacKenzie peered down into the dark abyss, and then looked at his men on both sides of the chasm. "Gentlemen, tomorrow we'll begin work on a newer, safer bridge. In the meantime, let's be rid of this one."

Lila squirmed and screamed as the men with the torches stepped forward. "Noooooo!"

Jay looked with frightened eyes at his father. Dr. Cooper looked back at both his children—Jay, hanging there like some helpless animal, and Lila, in the clutches of that beast.

On either side of the black abyss, the men set their torches to the remaining ropes of the bridge.

"Jesus!" Lila cried. "No, please!"

There was no time left for Jay to struggle. His father barely had time to pray. In just a moment the ropes burned through and snapped like very tired rubber bands, and the bridge—tangled victims, savage insects, and all—dropped like a broken, writhing necklace into the chasm.

Jay was gone. Dr. Cooper was gone. And Lila, as if stabbed through the heart, collapsed like a limp doll in the big guard's arms, her eyes closed in horror and anguish, her final scream only a weak, ebbing whimper.

MacKenzie looked down into the black hole, smiled, and then looked across the expanse at the trembling Lila.

"Prepare her for the Pit," he said.

EIGHT

It was a watery tornado, a tossing, tumbling, spinning, rumbling, thunderous carousel of water, black as
midnight, cold as stinging ice, fierce as a constantly
crashing tidal wave. Dr. Cooper and Jay were like tiny
splinters of driftwood, or helpless seaweed in the surf.
Their bodies were twisted, beaten, tossed about by
angry, merciless water. There was no air, there was no
surface, there was nowhere to swim.

There was only certain death.

Instinctively they were both holding what breath
they had left after smacking into the surface of the
churning water, but their lungs strained for air, and it
was all they could do to hold their mouths and noses
shut. *Air! Lord God, give us air!*

The water was carrying them somewhere, they
didn't know where, and in only a few more seconds it
wouldn't matter. They were prisoners in it, mere parti-
cles being swept along, the pressures and currents from
so many directions pummeling their bodies like heavy,
invisible hammers.

Jay could feel his brain blinking out. He was going
into a dream. Soon he would see Jesus. That was his

last thought before cold blackness and drifting, like sleep, like dreaming.

Pain! Salty stinging water. A heave of the stomach. Vomiting? No, coughing . . . hacking, more salty water spilling out, splashing on the wet, cold rocks. Water all around . . . someone's holding me.

Jay's eyes opened and saw nothing but a salty, briny, streaked blur of lights and colors. His eyes hurt and stung. His throat and windpipe felt like they were on fire. He gasped in one very painful, very congested, rattling breath, and then erupted with another horribly painful cough of foul, salty water that spit out in a spray upon the wet rock where he lay.

"Easy now," came the voice. "Just keep breathing. Do that first."

He drew another breath, and it hurt. He was thankful for the air, but it still hurt. His lungs were aching and burning, and he couldn't quit coughing. His eyes still saw nothing but a blur.

He heard someone else having a horrible fit of gasps and coughs, and it was his father. The voice just kept talking to them, telling them to relax and breathe, just breathe. They did that for a long time.

Jay could feel his head clearing up.

"Dad?" he asked very weakly and hoarsely.

"Yeah . . ." was the only answer he got, followed by more hacking and gasping.

"You're all right," said the voice. "I've got you. Just cough it up—that's the best thing."

Jay became aware of his arms. They could move. He reached with one hand and rubbed the brine and blur out of his eyes. He looked up.

Their rescuer was a kind-looking man with black, curly hair and a stocky build. He sat between Jay and his father, a hand hanging onto each of them, a kerosene lamp before him. He was soaking wet, and very concerned.

Jay looked at those kind eyes for a moment and then asked, "Did you . . . did you save us?"

The man nodded. "You made it through the whirlpool! The Lord was surely with you."

Jay shot a glance at his father. Dr. Cooper was looking up and smiling a wet and salty smile. He gathered enough strength to extend his cold, bluish hand and grip the man's arm.

"Reverend Adam MacKenzie?" Dr. Cooper asked.

"Yes!" exclaimed the man with a very sudden and great joy.

"Dr. Jake Cooper and his son Jay, on behalf of the International Missionary Alliance."

"You've . . . you've come to rescue me!" the man said.

Dr. Cooper looked like a drowned cat, and Jay looked no better. Both were very much aware of who had just saved who, and, wheezing or not, they couldn't help laughing a little.

"Jay," said Dr. Cooper, breathing easier now, "I'd liked to introduce you to Adam MacKenzie, the *real* one!"

Jay looked back and forth between his father and the real Adam MacKenzie, and he was full of questions.

The real Adam MacKenzie had a question of his own. "How did you know me?"

"I saw your picture in the desk of what's-his-name up there."

"Stuart Kelno?"

Dr. Cooper began picking himself up off the rocks. "That's the one."

Jay accepted Adam's helping hand as he stumbled to his feet. "Stuart Kelno?"

"Remember, Jay?" said Dr. Cooper. "Dulaney called him by that last name."

"But . . . but why would this Kelno character want to pretend he was Adam MacKenzie?"

The kind missionary was surprised and a little angry. "What's that? Stuart Kelno is pretending to be *me*?"

"Simply to throw us off so we wouldn't find you," said Dr. Cooper.

By now both Dr. Cooper and Jay could see clearly enough to let their eyes explore where they were, and they fell silent.

They stood in a huge cavern; the ceiling was at least a hundred feet above them, and the room seemed to stretch out in all directions like some immense, dark stadium made of black, crusty rock.

"We must be under the island," said Dr. Cooper.

"Yes," said Adam, "that's right. This is the center of the volcano that formed the island. All the lava is gone now, and so we have a huge, empty shell, sort of an upside-down cereal bowl."

Jay was curious. "So . . . what are you doing down *here*?"

Adam chuckled. "Oh, I got here the same way you did. Stuart Kelno's men threw me off that bridge up there, I went through the whirlpool, and here I am."

The Coopers looked behind them at the rushing river from which Adam had pulled them.

Jay asked, "So this is where all the water from that whirlpool goes?"

"Yes," answered Adam. "You see all the water over there, bubbling up from below that big wall? It rushes down underneath that wall and then comes up in this cavern and flows out to sea in this underground river. I just now happened to be doing some fishing when I saw your hat, Jacob, come bobbing up, and then both your heads." Adam smiled and handed Dr. Cooper his soggy hat. "I've done some lifesaving before. Both of you were very cooperative, I must say."

"We owe you our lives, Adam," said Dr. Cooper.

"And perhaps I'll owe you mine as well. I'm so glad you've come! Tommy must have gotten through with my note!"

Dr. Cooper shook his head sadly. "He was dead when his raft was found by a fishing vessel. The note was found in his pocket."

Adam was obviously stunned by the news and said nothing for several moments. Finally he asked, "Do you think this was Kelno's doing?"

"Absolutely. Have you heard of the curse called Moro-Kunda?"

Adam replied bitterly, "Yes, Kelno and his African tiger flies! I tried to expose that trick of his, but apparently he still makes good use of it."

"He told us that Tommy went crazy and tried to flee the island, but that he could not escape the curse. My guess is that Kelno planted a tiger fly in Tommy's provisions to silence him once he'd left."

"Tommy was one of my only remaining friends, one of the few who knew I was still alive down here. He kept it a secret, and did all he could to help me. His escape attempt was a desperate act, but he thought he might be able to find help. He carried that note on my behalf."

Adam forced himself to change the subject. "Listen, we all need to dry off, and you should get all the water out of your packs. Come up to my camp. I have a warm fire burning and some dry clothes."

But then Jay spotted something on the other side of some rocks, and he couldn't help exclaiming in surprise and wonderment, "Wow! Did *you* build that?"

Jay was referring to a very large boat, sitting beside the river on blocks of wood and stone. It was crudely built, and seemed to be constructed of countless different odds and ends of lumber, logs, and other scrap. The big hull looked like a deep, clumsy tub and a name was painted on the bow: "Adam's Ark."

"Yes, by the grace of God," answered Adam, "that's how I plan to get out of here. It's been my project for the last year or so."

"You've . . . you've been down here a *year?*" Dr. Cooper asked in amazement.

"Oh, I'm pretty sure it's been that long. There are no days or nights down here, so it's hard to tell."

They stepped up over the rough rocks, carrying their sodden backpacks, climbing away from the river until they reached a large shelf tucked up against the cavern wall. There, like some kind of subterranean Robinson Crusoe, Adam MacKenzie had built himself a rather quaint little camp spot, complete with a fire pit, a cot, several shelves for food, utensils, clothing, and tools, and several kerosene lamps that flooded the whole area and much of that part of the cavern with their warm yellow light.

Close by the camp, a stream of fresh, sparkling water splashed from a crack in the rocks above.

"My water supply," said Adam, "and my shower. Go ahead and rinse yourselves off."

The shower was a little cold, but it felt good! They all rinsed themselves and their clothes, and then wrapped their bodies in warm blankets while their clothes hung by the fire to dry. Adam prepared hot tea and biscuits from his store, and they shared a quick little meal together.

But the Coopers had only one thing on their minds.

"Kelno still has my daughter," said Dr. Cooper. "Is there any way back to the surface?"

Adam regretted his answer. "Well, there is, but I'm

afraid it won't be open for several more hours. You see, this river flows out from under the island through a very large tunnel, but most of the time the opening is underwater. It's only passable when the tide is low."

Dr. Cooper's mouth tightened, and he sighed forcefully. "We've got to get out of here! Lila's in great danger!"

Adam nodded sadly and with great concern. "I'm afraid that's a genuine possibility. Stuart Kelno is ruthless and claims power over this whole island. The Christian believers have all fled, and now he is totally free to do whatever he wants."

"The Christians have fled?" Jay asked, and then he recalled, "We saw a deserted village up there . . ."

Adam nodded. "That was our village. That was where the Lord first sent me, and He really blessed the work there. Almost all of the local natives in that village found Jesus as their Savior."

"What happened, Adam?" asked Dr. Cooper.

"Two things, I guess. First of all, Stuart Kelno and his followers came here and just—took over. They claimed to be followers of Jesus, and maybe they were sincere at first; but as Kelno got more and more fascinated with the island's pagan traditions he turned to Satanism and witchcraft, and his friends followed suit. So they took over all the resources and renamed the island Aquarius. Some of our own people, the ones who rejected the gospel, actually joined up with Kelno's bunch and continued their pagan practices."

"Firewalking?"

Adam looked a little sick as he said, "Yes, and somtimes human sacrifice to pagan gods, just like the heathen nations in the Old Testament. It was awful! Jacob, the people here were in terrible spiritual darkness before they found the Lord, and now some of them have been ensnared once again in the same old trap by this—this modern-age witch doctor! I pray for them every day."

"What was the other thing that happened?" Jay asked.

"Well, it's what's about to happen. I can always hope I'm wrong, but I think this island is in big trouble!"

"Your note!" said Jay. " 'The island is . . .' We couldn't make out the rest of it."

Adam looked at both of them and said in all seriousness, "This island, dear brothers, is *sinking*. It started very slowly a year ago, but since then it's been happening faster and faster. I'm afraid it could sink all at once, at any moment. I don't think there's much time left."

"Hmmmm," said Dr. Cooper. "So that's what Dulaney was talking about. . . ."

"Professor Dulaney?" asked Adam. "*Amos* Dulaney?"

"That's right. He tried to warn us about this, tried to get us to leave and take him with us."

Adam was stunned. "He used to be one of Kelno's chief advisors! He was the one who most strongly disagreed with me! He insisted nothing at all was happening to the island."

"Well, he changed his mind. Apparently his own findings convinced him you were right."

"What did Kelno think about that?"

"Well . . . I'm afraid Dulaney caught the curse of Moro-Kunda too."

Adam slapped his thigh angrily. "You see? You see? Satan is really using Kelno! This island is doomed, and I think Kelno even knows it, but he absolutely refuses to let anyone leave. All those people will *die*, Jacob! They will die when this island is destroyed, and it will be Kelno's doing!" He struggled with his feelings for a moment, and then continued. "The natives, the new Christians from the village, all left in canoes and rafts, anything they could find. They left behind all their earthly possessions. I remained here on the island, trying to warn the people still here, trying to reason with Kelno, trying to persuade some of the people who came from our village that they should leave with their families and not stay with this . . ."

"Antichrist?" suggested Dr. Cooper.

"A very descriptive term, Jacob," said Adam. "But they are still there with him, still deluded into thinking the Island of Aquarius is the perfect future for them all, a perfect place of peace and safety . . ."

Jay remembered a Bible verse. " '. . . but when they say "peace and safety," then sudden destruction will come upon them . . .' "

"Just as it will happen at the end of the age," Adam moaned. "They are so obsessed with Kelno's—and Satan's—lies that they refuse to listen to the truth. I tried to warn them, I tried to help them . . ."

"And they threw you off the bridge?" asked Dr. Cooper.

Adam nodded as tears filled his eyes. "Now all I can do is try to build this boat. Kelno has his own boat, but that means he controls all the transportation to and from the island. There is no escape from here except what we can build ourselves."

"So where did you get all those materials?" asked Jay.

"Well, it's sad, but all the lumber was originally brought to the island by the Missionary Alliance to build a church."

"Yes!" said Dr. Cooper. "I saw the blueprints and materials list in Kelno's desk. He apparently kept close tabs on every item."

"Every *stolen* item," Adam emphasized. "When the

villagers left, Kelno and his people ransacked and looted the village, taking everything they could find. I've
just been taking it back, board by board, nail by nail,
over the last several months."

The light dawned on Jay and Dr. Cooper.

"Ahhh . . ." said Dr. Cooper. "So you're the strange
thief who's been taking all those supplies!"

"Myself and a friend I still have up there. We never
could build a church, but . . . maybe this will be just as
good. We'll be saving lives either way."

Jay considered the meaning behind the name of the
boat. "Adam's Ark. I was wondering why it was so big!"

Dr. Cooper knew the answer as he asked, "You're
planning on passengers, aren't you?"

Adam just shrugged. "I'm a missionary."

The confinement hut was lonely, quiet, dismal. The
dark burn mark of a dead tiger fly was still upon the
floor. No matter. The madman might have failed then,
but now he had succeeded.

Dad and Jay were dead.

*Dear Lord, why? How could You let this happen? After
all the faith we put in You, after we've trusted You and seen
You protect us for so long, why? Why now?*

Lila lay motionless on her cot, too sick in her soul to
even pray. Would God hear her anyway? Was He really
even there anymore?

She wanted to close her eyes and just die right
there, but every time she shut her eyes, the scene came
back to her mind as vividly as when it happened. All
over again, she saw her father and brother dropping
helplessly, hopelessly into that roaring, gulping, watery
grave.

Lord, how can I ever trust You again?

She was startled from her shock and stupor by a

sound outside the door. It swung open and in came Candle, carrying a plate of food.

She looked up at him very dully. As far as she was concerned, she was dead already. How could anything matter anymore? Why bother being afraid?

But his eyes seemed so strangely kind toward her. They had such an odd look in them, something between sorrow and fear. He offered her the food. She only stared blankly at him.

He put the plate down and then knelt there beside the bed, trying to speak, trying to come up with some words.

"You . . . you papa . . ." he said, struggling, looking this way and that as if the words would come to him out of the air, or maybe from off the walls. "Me . . . Mee-Bwah!"

Lila wasn't interested in what this savage had to say.

Candle rattled on at her in his own words, so frantically and quickly that there was no hope of understanding a thing he was saying. But she couldn't help seeing the sincerity in his eyes. Was he truly concerned for her?

"What, Candle?" she finally asked quietly. "What are you trying to tell me?"

Then there were footsteps outside, and Candle quickly grabbed up the plate of food and stood there beside the cot, looking like his old, threatening, savage self.

In came the tyrant, the murderer, the antichrist, and oh, was he gloating, and smirking, and cutting her down to size with his eyes!

"Well, Miss Cooper," he said, swaggering back and forth and letting little chuckles hiss out through his nose, "I trust you are comfortable."

She spoke not a word.

"That's quite all right. I don't expect you to speak

to me. It must have been quite a horrible shock for you to find out how feeble your God really is. You know, I tried to warn your father time and again, but . . . oh, he was so brazen! Now you see, of course, that it was a very costly mistake! I would say his trust—and your trust—in this high and mighty God of yours was most severely misplaced!"

Lila glared up at him and spoke her latest bitter thought. "You aren't Adam MacKenzie at all, are you?"

He laughed loudly and rudely. "No, no, my child, no! I only led you to believe I was the late Reverend MacKenzie so you would be satisfied that you'd found him and leave the island with a good report. I had no idea you would be so snoopy and persistent! No, actually the name is Stuart Kelno. *Lord* Stuart Kelno, the last and ultimate prophet! This is my world, my creation. Here, on Aquarius, *I* am God!"

"You'll never be God," said Lila. "You can pretend all you want, but there is only one God, and someday you'll have to answer to Him for killing my father and brother!"

He only smiled mockingly at her. "Amusing. From the performance of your God thus far, I would not think He was capable of any kind of authority over someone as powerful as I. But do tell me: just what is your God going to do to set you free from my will?" Kelno leaned close to Lila, and she could smell his breath. "Go ahead. Cry out to Him! See if He'll strike me with lightning! See if He'll overpower me somehow!"

He sat regally on the opposite cot and looked at her, his evil eyes glistening with delight. "No doubt you must be wondering what's to become of you. Well, we do have a formal occasion planned at sunrise. You'll have to dress up. Some ladies will be in soon to take care of that." Then he stood up and towered over her proudly. "Yes, quite a prize, quite a prize indeed!" He glanced at the plate of food in Candle's hand. "Well, are you going to eat anything?"

Lila couldn't answer. She just couldn't talk to this beast.

The beast hated being ignored. He snapped at Candle, "Take it away then!"

Candle hesitated. He looked at Lila with pain in his eyes.

"*Take it away!*"

Candle obeyed, and the two men left the hut, locking and bolting the door behind them.

"Brrr!" said Jay, pulling his blanket more tightly around him. "There's a draft!"

The smoke from the fire was beginning to move sideways. It was all a little new and strange because up until now there had not been any movement of air at all in this very dead, very still place.

"Oh," said Adam, "the tide is beginning to drop below the tunnel entrance. Fresh air is coming in from outside."

"Fresh air—" said Dr. Cooper.

"That means we can get out of here!" said Jay.

Adam only shook his head. "My canoe isn't here at the moment, and it would be useless to try to swim."

"The air . . ." Dr. Cooper muttered. "The air . . . it's moving."

"Well," said Adam, "sure. It's a good thing, too. I'd suffocate in here if I didn't get a daily change of air from outside."

"But there's a current of air!" said Dr. Cooper, jumping up. "Jay, get dressed!"

Jay jumped up and grabbed his clothes. "What is it, Dad?"

"That air blowing in here! It would never do that unless it had someplace to go. It's circulating, which means it must be escaping somewhere."

The three of them dressed in a mad rush as the cool air continued to move over their bodies. They could feel it very plainly now.

"We'll have to follow it," said Dr. Cooper.

He looked at the smoke from the little fire, and now it was wafting away sideways, moving up the sides of the cavern. He started following it, darting so quickly over the rocks that Jay and Adam struggled to keep up.

"Have you ever noticed any vents, or tunnels, or lava shafts, anything like that?" Dr. Cooper asked over his shoulder.

"Oh . . . well, yes, but I never gave it much thought," said Adam.

"Where?"

Adam pointed to a small nook far up the wall. The climb was steep, but possible.

"We'll need lanterns," said Dr. Cooper.

Jay and Adam brought two lanterns, and Adam got a pick and shovel as well.

"I have to warn you, Jacob," said Adam. "This tunnel, this shaft, could be inhabited. During the times when the air is still, I can smell something up in there, and sometimes I've heard noises."

But that only made Dr. Cooper more excited. He looked at Jay with a wonderful new realization, and Jay looked back at him blankly.

Dr. Cooper said to Adam, "You mean there could be some kind of creature in there?"

"Well, yes," Adam said, "and from the local folklore on this island, I don't think it's the kind of creature we'd want to encounter."

"Do the local natives worship it?"

"Oh, yes! With great fear! They still offer human sacrifices to it."

Dr. Cooper was nearly wild with excitement. "The Pit! Jay, remember the Pit up above? It looked like it could be some sort of volcanic vent. We may be able to reach it from below!"

"Let's go!" said Jay.

"Wait!" said Adam. "Are you sure you know what you're doing?"

"When do the sacrifices take place?" Dr. Cooper asked.

"At the rising of the sun," said Adam. "Just a few hours." Then he realized something. "You think . . . you think Kelno will let them use *Lila*. . . ?"

"What do *you* think?"

Adam turned pale. "I think we'd better hurry!"

NINE

They climbed higher and higher, stepping carefully over the rough volcanic rocks until they came to the place Adam had pointed out.

By now there was a very brisk wind blowing, and as they followed it they easily found several small openings in the rocks. Some were large holes, some were mere cracks, but all were sucking the air like a vacuum. The men spread out, checking here and there, trying to find whatever hole might be the best bet as a passage.

"Dad, how about this one?" Jay called.

They were all there immediately. The light from their lanterns shone into a very large passageway which, by the sound of the echoes, had to go back inside the island for a long distance.

"Yes, this could be it. Let's see if we can move some of these rocks."

The three worked together with the pick and shovel and their bare hands and managed to nudge some of the·rocks aside. Finally the passage was opened wide enough. They clambered inside.

"Yes," said Dr. Cooper, peering ahead in the light of the lanterns. "An old lava vent. This tube could lead us clear to the surface."

They started walking, climbing, crawling, squeezing through the passageway as it curled and worked its way upward through the core of the island like some gigantic burrow. The island's core was a bizarre place; they seemed to be crawling along through a huge black sponge, with openings on every side, dangerous holes to step around, low overhangs to crouch under. They tried to follow the main lava vent as it meandered upward, but sometimes it was difficult to choose which way to go. The movement of the air was their best guide. Whenever they found themselves in an area with dead, still air, they knew they had made a wrong turn. They would double back to where they again could feel the air moving upward through the tube.

Dr. Cooper crawled up a long, narrow chute of rock, onto a level area high above. He called to Jay and Adam, "Say, take a look at this!"

They too climbed up through the chute, the echoes of their labored breathing taking on deep, throaty tones as if they were inside a huge bell. They reached the level area where Dr. Cooper was waiting, and he immediately pointed out something in the sandy floor of the tunnel.

"Oh-oh . . ." said Jay.

"Maybe this was caused by your creature," said Dr. Cooper.

They saw a strange, deep groove in the sand, as if something very large had been dragged through it. There was also a very obvious and disagreeable smell.

"Dad, is your gun okay?" Jay asked.

"Maybe," he answered. "I rinsed it and dried it, but I don't have any oil for it, and as for the cartridges, well, they did make a trip underwater."

"Lord," prayed Adam, "please keep us safe."

"Amen to that," said Dr. Cooper.

Suddenly the many cavities and passages all around them began to echo with groans, crumbles, and loud creaks. They braced themselves against the rough stone walls. They could feel the whole island moving, quaking, wrenching. The sound was horrible, deafening. They felt as if they were trapped inside a huge rock crusher.

Adam started praying out loud, bracing himself in a cranny in the rocks. Jay tried to keep his lantern from breaking. Dr. Cooper kept turning this way and that, trying to observe what was happening. They could actually feel it: a strange, falling sensation like riding downwards in a very jerky elevator.

"It's getting worse!" cried Adam. "The island's shell is collapsing!"

They could hear loud cracklings like explosions booming and rippling up through the many pores and crevices in the earth; somewhere, far below, giant cracks were bursting open. The rocks were splitting.

Then, as the other sounds died down a little and the shaking subsided, a new noise worked its way up to their ears from far, far below. It was the sound of rushing water.

"Do you hear that?" asked Adam.

Dr. Cooper nodded. "The sea is breaking through into the island's foundations."

"It will erode away whatever base the island still has to rest upon!"

"We only have a matter of hours!" said Dr. Cooper, hurrying upward through the tube. "Let's go!"

Lila felt the shaking as well, as did all the residents of Stuart Kelno's kingdom. They were clearly alarmed and worried about it, but as far as Lila could tell, they were determined to believe whatever Kelno told them.

"It is the spiritual forces of the island," said the pretty Polynesian woman who was combing Lila's hair.

"Lord Kelno says the spirits are grieved because their private sanctuary has been invaded by outsiders."

"Myself and my family, in other words," said Lila, grudgingly allowing the woman to put flowers in her hair.

Another woman, a witchy-looking old crone from the island's bygone days, was preparing a long gown of white linen.

"Ah, but in the morning we will appease them," she said, holding the gown out to Lila.

"What's this, a tablecloth?" Lila asked sarcastically.

"It is your cermonial gown," said the pretty woman. "You must be dressed correctly to be presented to Kudoc!"

"Who is Kudoc?" Lila asked, certain she would not like the answer.

The old witch's eyes lit up with awe as she answered, "Kudoc is the Lord of All Nature, the Serpent God of the Underworld! He lives deep beneath us, and the island quakes with his anger!"

No, Lila certainly did not like that answer. "Serpent God? Where? What are you going to do?"

The old woman only threw the gown over Lila's head, saying, "Quickly. Put this on."

Lila hesitated for just a moment, and then slipped the gown over her hiking fatigues. For now, there was nothing else to do but go along with all this distasteful pagan nonsense. *Lord God*, she prayed, *please grant me the right moment, the right opportunity, the chance to get free, throw off this silly gunnysack, and run!*

"Soon we will go to the Sacred Pit," said the old woman, observing the brightening of the eastern sky.

The disagreeable smell was stronger now. Dr. Cooper was thinking more and more about his gun, and he tried to keep his right hand unoccupied. Deep below, and all around them, they could still hear low rumbles from the quivering, settling, crumbling island.

"How much further could it be?" Jay had to ask.

"Hssst!" said Dr. Cooper, stopping short and holding up his hand. They all froze.

Adam looked over Dr. Cooper's shoulder, and Jay looked around him, and then all three could see what had stopped Dr. Cooper: off to the right, through a low opening, was a small cavern. "Looks like a nest," said Dr. Cooper very quietly.

They moved in slow motion, coming closer, letting the light of the lanterns penetrate further into the cavern. They saw more sand, then some bones. They could smell many strong, sickening odors.

The main lava vent went right by that opening. There was no way to sneak around it. And, just coming into view, peeking out from behind the cave wall, was something white, smooth, and round.

They all knew what it was. A huge egg.

They were dealing with some kind of reptile.

Another step. The light from the lanterns now illumined a large, cavernous room, the bone-strewn lair of some very large, very gruesome creature.

"Whatever it is," said Dr. Cooper, "it isn't home."

"But look at the size of that egg!" said Jay. "It's as big as a watermelon!"

Adam observed, "The parent must be large enough to easily . . . uh . . . swallow a human . . ." As soon as he said that, he realized he shouldn't have. Dr. Cooper was gone like a shot up the tunnel. Jay and Adam ran to catch up with him.

The fiery sun peeked from behind the distant horizon, turning the ocean blood-red. A strange, solemn stillness lay over the entire village. From somewhere in the jungle a single drumbeat began to pound, pound, pound, like a headache.

Lila was on her knees when two native guards came in. *Jesus, I'm ready to be with You,* she was praying. *It will all be for the better anyway; I'll be with Dad and Jay, and that's what I want most of all. Just . . . please, don't let it hurt too much.*

Before she knew it, her hands were bound behind her and she was being led along between two very large Polynesians in regal-looking feathers, shells, and skins. They walked down the main road through the village as the followers of Stuart Kelno, young, old, male, and female, all appeared and followed them in a long, solemn parade, heading up the road and then turning down that forbidden trail, drawn by the steady, pulsing, beating drum.

Jay and Adam came to an abrupt halt and even took a few quick steps backward, grabbing onto any available handhold.

"What now?" said Dr. Cooper, coming up from behind.

"The end of the line, maybe," said Adam.

Jay and Adam allowed Dr. Cooper to squeeze between them in the narrow tunnel and have a look for himself.

Incredibly, the earth had split apart as if cut with a knife. Dr. Cooper looked down, sideways, and above them at a huge rift, a jagged chasm that reached high above them and dropped away into bottomless blackness beneath. Some thirty feet away, across the chasm, the lava tunnel continued like a hole in a slice of bread.

"This happened recently!" Dr. Cooper observed.

"Look at those clean surfaces, and those fragments still crumbling off."

"Hang on!" Jay exclaimed.

He hollered because he was the only one who could think of it. All three backed away from the edge of that split in a hurry.

The ground was shaking and heaving again, and the chasm was moving. It was creaking and groaning; the walls were shifting, quivering, and rumbling together a little, and then apart again, as more fragments of rock broke loose and tumbled down into blackness. As the Coopers and Adam MacKenzie watched in horror and awe, the opposite wall of the rift swayed toward them, and then away from them, first just a few feet, then several feet, back and forth.

"What now?" Jay asked.

"It might . . . it might draw in close enough." Dr. Cooper considered.

"You—you don't mean we're going to jump across!" Adam exclaimed.

"I'll let you know in a second."

The solemn parade of pagans finally reached the ominous clearing with all the altar stones, the drooping, mournful trees, and, of course, the Pit.

Stuart Kelno was there already, standing near it with some old native witch doctors who beat a drum and looked perfectly hideous under many feathers and much bright paint. He looked at Lila gloatingly.

The two big Polynesians led her to the edge of the Pit, the many people gathered all around, and then the drumming came to a sudden, dead stop. The silence was numbing. Not a single toe or finger stirred. Lila looked around at all the people, who seemed oddly pleased and proud of her. Many were smiling, as if it were her birthday or her high school graduation.

Kelno looked her up and down, admiring the flowers in her hair and the beautiful gown. "You look absolutely breathtaking, Miss Cooper!" he said.

Everyone applauded.

All Lila could do was stare into that yawning pit and consider the many bones still lying down there. *Lord, please keep me cool. Don't let me fall apart! Please show me the way out of this!*

The opposite wall of that jagged rift shuddered, and backed away, shedding some more loose fragments and finally coming to rest in one place for a moment.

"Come on, come on," pled Dr. Cooper.

With another shaking and another deep rumble, the wall began to move again, drawing in closer. Closer. Closer!

The chasm was now twenty feet across.

The wall began to move back.

"No!" said Dr. Cooper. "Lord, please!"

A violent shaking again! All around them the earth seemed to cry and roar in pain as the island's insides split and crumbled.

The wall heaved toward them. The chasm tightened to fifteen feet. Ten. Eight.

Jay handed his lantern to his father, took several steps backward, and braced himself.

The wall began to move outward again.

"Go!" Dr. Cooper yelled.

Jay shot forward, took a flying leap from the very edge of the chasm, sailed out over the infinite, black space below him, and landed on the other side.

The chasm was widening again!

"Go!" Dr. Cooper yelled to Adam.

Adam set down his lantern, took a run at it, and with a scream of terror and determination sailed through the air to the other side, where Jay grabbed him and pulled him to safety.

The island shook and rumbled angrily.

"Be calm!" Stuart Kelno shouted to his troubled followers.

Many were hanging on to each other and some were even on the ground, unable to stand up because of the shaking. The mournful trees swayed back and forth, reeling from the lurching ground. Even the witch doctors were wide-eyed with fear and chattering among themselves.

Kelno raised his hands for attention and silence, and said, "The spirits and forces of the Island of Aquarius have been violated, and this is the result. This is a good lesson for all of us, and let us pay heed to it. But fear not. Since it is the spirits of this island who are offended, then let the old traditions of this island now appease them." He turned to the witch doctors and said, "You may proceed according to your customs."

With eerie cries, bellows, and chanting, the witch doctors started pounding their drums again. Lila winced at the racket and knew it was all demonic, pure witchcraft to its very core.

"Lord Jesus," she prayed, "I plead Your shed blood over me to protect me from Satan's wiles. If I must die, then so be it. I know I'll be with You. But . . . if it's okay with You, I really don't want Satan to win."

There was no more time to pray. Suddenly the two big guards whipped some ropes around her, binding her legs and arms close to her body, and then, as a cheer went up from natives and newcomers alike, Lila was lowered by a rope into the Pit. Down, down, one arm's length of rope at a time, her body scraping against the rocks, turning slowly as the rope twisted, dropping closer and closer to that eerie, disgusting bed of bones below. The shouts and cheers of the people above echoed all around her like angry bats.

Her feet touched the sandy bottom, but she had no balance and no use of her tightly bound arms and legs. With a gasp and a rustling of her linen gown, she flopped down onto the floor of the Pit, her body flipping a few rib bones aside, her head punching a shallow dish in the sand. She found herself face-to-face with an old, sun-bleached skull, its empty sockets ever-staring, its crooked teeth grinning with mocking delight.

She was trying to think, and to pray, and very desperately trying not to cry.

TEN

Dr. Cooper was about to jump across the perilous, shifting chasm. He had already tossed the lanterns across to Jay and Adam, and now he waited for the right moment to make his attempt.

But as the earth continued to reel and shift and the chasm yawned wider, all three men could see a very small glimmer of daylight high above them, far up inside the rift. The horrible split had cut through the entire island, clear to the surface.

Then they heard a loud clatter above, followed by crashing and splintering. As the three men watched from both sides of the chasm, dirt, rocks, chunks of concrete, splintered lumber, shattered glass, pieces of wall, and even the remains of a few chairs dropped past them like garbage down a chute, disappearing with a great commotion into the deep recesses far below. Soon they could hear distant splashes as the falling debris and junk hit the inpouring seawater.

"I think part of a house just went by," said Dr. Cooper.

"I think you'd better jump, Dad," Jay suggested nervously.

"Stand back."

Dr. Cooper took off his hat and threw it over the

chasm. Then he took off his boots and tossed them across. He got back as far as he could in the tunnel and then, running faster than he had for a long time, he bounded for the precipice, launched out across the chasm, sailed through the air, and . . . he made it! He pitched forward and rolled on the rocks, but he made it.

"Boy, I haven't done that since high school," he remarked.

Dr. Cooper put on his boots and his hat, the three of them gathered up their gear, and away they went.

The drumbeats stopped. The chanting and cheering and wailing stopped. Lila was still lying helplessly on the floor of the Pit. With her face half in the sandy floor, she could not look up, but she could hear the people leaving. This must be a very sacred event, too sacred for anyone to remain and watch.

So now what? *I can't move,* Lila thought, *I'm all alone in the bottom of this hole, and apparently something is on its way to eat me.*

But the Lord was certainly with her. Lila was amazed that she was not more terrified. This had to be the ultimate terror, the most horrible way in the world to die, and yet she still felt a very sure and familiar peace about the whole thing.

"You *do* hear my prayers, don't You?" she said aloud.

And the Lord seemed to answer her right away. Besides the peace, she began to feel something else: suddenly she was filled with a desire to fight, as if a holy anger welled up inside her. She began to wriggle and squirm.

"Lord," she prayed, "I'm ready if You are. I'm going to do whatever I can. And, Satan, you can just lump it!"

The volcanic rocks were rough and abrasive. She rolled over on her back and raised her feet up, resting her bound ankles against the rock wall of the Pit. There. She started scraping up and down, rubbing the rope against the rocks.

Lila could feel a breeze from somewhere wafting over her face. But it wasn't a fresh breeze at all. It carried a terrible smell.

She kept rubbing.

"Oh, great!" said Dr. Cooper.

The tunnel had suddenly branched into two passages.

"Should we split up?" asked Jay.

"No, no, it's too dangerous," his father answered. Then he looked at his watch. "It's morning up there."

Adam choked back some horrible fears. "There may not be any more time!"

Dr. Cooper bent down and carefully examined the floor of each tunnel. In the right tunnel, he found nothing. In the left tunnel, he looked closer; then he went in deeper.

"All right," he said, "this is it."

He pointed out the familiar grooved pattern in the floor of the tunnel. The creature had been this way.

They hurried along, ducking under low rocks and around tight corners, their hearts pounding with a steadily rising fear.

Lila made a face. What was that smell? It seemed to be getting worse. She kept working at the rope around her ankles, scraping, scraping, scraping.

Snap! Her legs were free. She kicked and wriggled and worked the rope loose. Then she finally got her legs under her and stood up.

Sssssssss.

Oh no. What was that sound?

Sssss. . . .

It seemed to be coming from behind that boulder over there. There must be an opening.

Come on, Lila, get the ropes off!

She backed against the rocks and started scraping at the rope that tied her wrists. Up, down, up, down, frantically digging away at each fiber. Was she even cutting through the rope?

The smell was stronger now. Something was causing it, all right, and that something was getting closer.

Sssssssss . . .

Lord, help me cut this rope!

Jay hurried through a tight passage ahead of Adam and Dr. Cooper. Suddenly his feet dropped through the floor. All around him, the floor of the tunnel turned into shards and pebbles that tumbled down a deep, vertical shaft, bounding and clattering off the sides.

A strong hand grabbed his shirt-sleeve, and then another hand got a better grip on his arm.

"Hang on, son, hang on!" Dr. Cooper shouted.

Jay didn't kick and struggle. He knew better than that. But he could hear the echo of a very deep well under his dangling feet, and it was all he could do to keep from panicking.

Dr. Cooper pulled on Jay, and Adam pulled on Dr. Cooper, and finally they got Jay back on solid ground.

Dr. Cooper held his lantern high for a better look. "Just like a trap! The floor was paper-thin just over that lava shaft. Looks like we can make it around the shaft on that ledge over there."

They started inching along the one-foot ledge, their backs to the wall, the deep well right at their feet.

Ssssssssssss . . .

The thing was getting closer. Lila kept working at the rope. It had to be getting thinner by now!

She could hear a new sound: a long, drawn-out, hissing noise like breathing. Something was slithering, sliding through the rocky crevices. "Come on, rope, break!"

A foul puff of hot, wet air blew into the Pit. Lila looked toward the opening. Her heart turned over in her chest.

Just emerging from the darkness were two huge, golden, glistening eyes, rising higher and higher out of the opening.

The eyes focused on her. There was another puff of moist air from the thing's nostrils.

It had spotted her.

ELEVEN

"Jesus!" Lila prayed, and suddenly, snap! The rope broke. She worked it loose and brought her arms around.

The glowing eyes emerged from the opening, and a monstrous, dragonlike head crept into the light. It was . . . a *snake!* But how could any snake be so enormous? The head itself was as big as a huge alligator's head, supported on a long, leathery neck the size of a tree trunk. A slimy tongue whipped about in the air, and hot, steamy breath chugged out of the nostrils.

It was still glaring at her, but seemed in no real hurry. Apparently it was accustomed to finding regular, easy meals in this trap. The thick body kept pouring into the pit as the big head reared up and towered over Lila like an armless dinosaur, swaying back and forth, the tongue licking in and out.

Lila bent and grabbed a long piece of bone. She had no idea what to do with it, but she wasn't about to let this beast have her without some kind of fight.

Aww! What was that? Lila ducked backwards, startled by something that dropped right on her head. It was a rope!

The snake lunged at her! She ducked and burrowed into the bones on the sandy floor. The snake's big snout thudded against the stone wall. She wriggled her body, faced upward, and saw that she was lying right under the snake's swaying, white-scaled neck. She was out of its range of vision, and it had lost her. The big head coiled around, the nostrils snuffing angrily, the tongue tasting the air for her scent. The big eyes caught sight of her again.

Someone screamed from above, "Come! You come, girl!"

The snake lunged again. Lila half expected it; she dropped suddenly, but held the bone up. The snake jammed the round end of the bone against the wall and the jagged end into its snout. A hiss of pain exploded from that deep, cotton-white mouth. Lila dove under its arching neck, crawling toward the dangling rope. The snake whipped its head back and forth, trying to shake the bone out of its leathery hide.

Lila grabbed the rope, which immediately jerked her upward. The floor of the pit dropped away.

No! The snake had clamped its jaws on her gown. It was pulling her down!

She screamed. "Candle!"

The big Polynesian was up above, pulling with all his might on the rope.

Lord, help me!

The snake jerked and twisted its head, throwing Lila about on the end of the rope. But then the gown began to rip away. Lila dropped one arm and let it tear and slip down over her shoulder. The snake pulled and yanked, and finally got itself a mouthful of linen.

Lila shot upward out of the Pit and into the strong arms of Candle. Quickly he set her aside and out of danger, and then he grabbed up a very large slab of raw meat and threw it at the snake.

Lila saw the huge head shoot out of the pit, its

mouth wide open, and the meat vanished down that hungry, gulping throat as blood dripped over the jaws.

Candle grabbed Lila's hand, and they ran. She asked no questions. She just ran and ran.

"I think I see daylight," said Adam.

The three of them hurried toward it, and then froze.

A long, slithering tail with thick, leathery skin lay in the tunnel like a huge log.

They backed away, horrified, speechless. Dr. Cooper had his gun ready, but . . . what good could it possibly do against something so monstrous?

The tail whipped about! The thing began to move!

They ducked into a tiny hollow in the rocks, the only possible hiding place.

With a long scraping against the rocks and over the sand, the big leathery log slid up through the tunnel, curled, and turned around. Then the snake's enormous, ugly dinosaur-head passed by them, blood still apparent on the jaws as the monster slithered down into the depths of the quaking island.

Each man was thinking about that blood, and what it could mean, but no one would say anything about it. No word could be encouraging. They waited until the tail thinned to a point and vanished into the catacombs below, and then they retraced the path of the snake upward toward the daylight until they broke through the opening.

It was the Pit. They had reached it. There was no sign of Lila. Or was there?

When they spotted the white linen gown, it was Adam who approached it slowly, stepping over and through the scattered bones. With just two fingers he gingerly picked it up. He did not turn around.

"What is it?" Dr. Cooper asked.

"It's a . . . it's . . ."

"What is it?" Dr. Cooper asked again.

"It's a ceremonial gown," Adam finally forced himself to say. "It's used for . . ."

Dr. Cooper was there, snatching the gown from him.

"It's used in the sacrifices," Adam finished saying.

Dr. Cooper looked at the gown carefully. It was stained with blood. He held it by the shoulders and let it drape downward. It was Lila's size.

"Dad—" said Jay, picking something out of the sand.

It was a small gold cross on a fine chain, Lila's favorite, the one she always wore around her neck.

"This doesn't mean—" Adam started to say.

"No!" said Dr. Cooper desperately. "It doesn't!" His voice was very strained. "It can't!"

Jay could only lean against the rock wall, his body limp, his face pale.

Dr. Cooper folded the little gown once, twice, again, gathering it up in his trembling hands. He held it close to his chest, and then he just stood there, motionless, for a long time.

"Dad . . ." Jay tried to say, but his throat was so dry and his voice so weak he could hardly get it out. "We don't really know."

Dr. Cooper stood there, motionless and silent.

From deep below, the rumbling started again. The earth quivered a little.

Adam remembered. "Jacob . . . the lowest tide will be in two hours. It may be the only chance we'll have to get the boat out through the tunnel and away from here before the island collapses. Jacob, do you hear me?"

Dr. Cooper did not look like he heard anything.

Adam spoke again, very gently. "Jacob, we must try to warn these people. We must try to save them. We must do it, Jacob."

Jay awoke from his shock and stupor enough to say, "I—I don't understand any of this. Who is there to save, Adam? These people . . . they don't deserve it. Just look at what they've done!"

"God loves them. He saved *us,* Jay, and *we* didn't deserve it. We must share His love with them as well."

Jay fidgeted and looked at the bone-strewn ground. "You're just saying that because you're a missionary."

Adam touched Dr. Cooper's arm and looked with compassionate eyes at Jay. "Aren't we all?"

Suddenly Dr. Cooper came alive again, drawing a deep breath and looking all around at the walls. "We'll have to form a human ladder to get out of here. Between the three of us we should be able to do it."

But Adam saw something in Dr. Cooper's eyes he greatly feared. "Jacob, are you all right?"

"I'll be the bottom man. Adam, get on my shoulders."

Adam hesitated.

"Get on my shoulders, Adam!" Dr. Cooper ordered.

Adam was worried, but he complied. Jay then climbed up to Adam's shoulders and was able to reach the ground above. He immediately found a rope. He did wonder where it came from, but there was no time to ponder it. Within moments he had secured one end to a large altar stone. Dr. Cooper and Adam climbed out.

Dr. Cooper's eyes were hard and cold, and set resolutely toward the village. "They may be eating their morning meal about now, and they'll be off guard. Jay, we might need to try a diversionary ploy."

"Jacob," Adam said, his voice full of concern, "are you sure about your motives?"

"Let's get going!" Dr. Cooper answered, thumbing the hammer and turning the chambers on his gun.

Lila kept running, following the massive Polynesian over winding, nearly overgrown trails and through thick vegetation and gooey marshes. She was so exhilarated at being alive that she didn't think she could ever get tired.

They came to that obscure trail he had shown them earlier, the one that led to the half-sunken village. They raced down it, ending up at that same village. Candle led the way up a small hill to a single hut still safely above the rising waters. Lila looked toward the sea and noticed that the village was now completely gone under the restless, foaming surf.

"What. . . !" she exclaimed. "What's happened?"

Candle pulled her into the hut, and then the two of them collapsed on the soft dirt floor to catch their breath.

"Why did you do that?" Lila asked. "Why did you save me?"

She asked the question a few times, nearly reenacting the event to get him to understand. Candle desperately tried to answer, but could not find the words. Finally he reached down with his finger and etched out a Christian cross in the dirt.

"Mee-Bwah!" he said, and then pointed to his heart.

Lila understood that right away, and she wondered . . . "You . . . you know *Jesus?*"

"Mee-Bwah!" he said, poking the palms of his hands

to imitate nail wounds and then pressing his palms together as if praying. "Jesus! Mee-Bwah!"

Lila could not believe it. She could feel the joy washing over her! "Candle, you really know Jesus?"

He nodded, and then said, "Adam."

"Adam? You mean, Adam MacKenzie?"

"Adam, he Mee-Bwah."

"Adam is a Christian?" Lila pointed at the cross in the dirt to make sure she was following what Candle was saying. Candle nodded with a big smile. "And he told you about Jesus?" Lila poked her palms as she said the name, and Candle nodded again. "But where is Adam MacKenzie? Is he dead?"

Candle shook his head. "No! No dead! Adam . . ." Candle ran out of words, and started scratching out a picture in the dirt. He drew a crude sketch of the chasm with the whirlpool, and even made whirlpool noises with his mouth. He then pantomimed how Adam fell into the whirlpool.

"Oh, no," Lila said. "Then—he's dead, just like . . ." She could not continue. She was choking up with tears.

But Candle would not let her cry. He waved his hand in front of her face to get her attention, hollering, "No! No dead! Adam!" He drew a simple diagram of the cavern under the island, then scratched in a little stick figure of a man, pointed at it, and said again, "Adam!"

Lila used gestures to ask, "There is a . . . a cavern under the island?"

Candle nodded.

"And Adam is down there alive?"

"You papa, maybe. Big papa, little papa!"

"My father and brother."

Candle nodded.

Lila felt like she was going into shock again. Alive? Jay and Dad alive? "How . . . how do I get to them?" she asked.

Candle threw back his head and laughed. He leaped to his feet and beckoned to her to follow. Out the door they went, running further up the hill to another hut, a very large one. It must have been a meeting hall at one time. They ducked inside.

Lila couldn't believe her eyes. This primitive hut in the jungle had been turned into a warehouse. The hut was filled with lumber, supplies, cans of gasoline, tools, and—several crates from the Coopers' own boat, safe and sound, rescued from being burned!

"Candle," said Lila, making a quick, mental inventory of everything, "how did all this stuff get here?"

Candle grinned widely and pointed at himself.

It dawned on Lila. "*That's* what you were doing every night! You were sneaking this stuff away from Kelno's village."

He understood enough to nod his head again and laugh at his own cleverness.

Lila had to laugh too. "We found your torch on a rock in the jungle."

"But Candle *here!*"

"But why have you been saving all this stuff?"

"Adam."

"Even the supplies from our boat?"

"No. *You* stuff! Candle take you stuff. No burn. You keep."

Lila was very grateful. She took his hand. "Thank you, Candle. That was very brave of you. You could have been caught trying to help us."

He didn't understand everything she said, but he knew she was saying thank you, so he bowed and nodded.

Lila was awestruck. She closed her eyes and said, "Thank You, Lord. You've answered my prayer."

"Mee-Bwah," said Candle, looking heavenward.

In the village, fully awake now, sounds of breakfast were coming up the street from the dining hall.

But there were other sounds, booming and rumbling like threatening thunder from deep under the island. The quivering could be felt in one's feet; the shifting and rocking could be seen in the tall trees. There was a creeping tension in the air, and an inescapable fear pervaded every heart.

On Lord Kelno's orders, a lawyer and a bricklayer stood as lonely, frightened sentries at the village entrance, hearing, feeling, and discussing the sounds and the shakings and what they could mean. Lord Kelno had said the tremors would cease once the last of the intruders was destroyed, offered to the Serpent God, but there had been no relief from the rumblings and the quaking ground. If anything, it had all become worse, and though neither man would say it out loud, each was sure that even Lord Kelno himself was frightened. If not the quakes, then certainly he feared those strange, American visitors with their old, outdated, Christian religion. After all, they thought, if Lord Kelno is so sure they are dead and gone forever, why did he order us to stand guard here in broad daylight?

As the two stood at their posts, rifles on their shoulders, they spoke in very hushed tones about their fears and their doubts. The earth had already opened up and devoured a house. What next? Where? Who would be the victim?

Suddenly there were footsteps! They were coming up the trail toward the village. A figure appeared out of the jungle. The two sentries froze. What was this? A spirit? A trick of their minds?

There, on the trail as if he owned it, was the image, the ghost, the spirit of that young intruder, that young Cooper boy!

Should they speak to it? What good would their guns do?

"H-halt there, whoever you are!" said the lawyer.

The spirit said not a word, but only smiled and kept walking toward them.

They raised their rifles to aim, but at the same time they backed away, visibly terrified.

The spirit kept coming.

All it took was that one brief moment of fear and indecision for two more apparitions to drop down on the guards from trees on either side of the road. Before either man knew what had happened, the "ghosts" of Adam MacKenzie and Jacob Cooper had wrestled them to the ground and taken their rifles away from them.

"Good work, Jay," said Dr. Cooper, emptying the cartridges out of one man's rifle.

"What now?" asked Adam, emptying the other rifle.

"We go for the kingpin," said Dr. Cooper. "Lord Kelno."

"What are you going to do?" asked the sentries, quite intimidated.

Dr. Cooper still was not answering that kind of question. He just looked at the two men and demanded, "Where can I find him?"

The two men looked at each other and then one answered, "In his cottage. But he's surrounded by his bodyguards. You'll never get to him."

"We'll see." Dr. Cooper's eyes were cold and determined. "Come on, on your feet. We'll need you two along for a little insurance."

With the two unwilling sentries walking ahead, the three men stole down the main street, their eyes alert, their footsteps silent and stealthy. They were coming close to the dining hall. All the people were inside trying to eat, all listening to the rumblings and gripping the sides of their tables with white-knuckled hands.

"Adam, they just might be ready to listen to you," Dr. Cooper observed.

They came to the edge of the village square, and they could see the lights burning in Stuart Kelno's cottage. Two sentries sat on the veranda, eating their breakfast from paper plates and not entirely alert for intruders.

"Wait here," said Dr. Cooper.

Adam was about to ask a question—but Dr. Cooper was suddenly gone!

Like a bullet from a rifle, like a cougar pouncing on its prey, Dr. Cooper shot across the village square and bounded up the cottage steps before either sentry could even realize what was happening. One thug managed to grab his rifle, but a powerful hand rammed into him and flung his whole body against the wall. He was out of the game. The other sentry only had time to take one step forward before a boot caught him in the center of the chest and propelled him over the rail.

Two down.

The cottage door burst open, tearing the hinges loose. The bodyguard in the living room only saw a blur that dove into his stomach like a torpedo, pitching him backward over a couch and through the rear window. He was out.

Three down.

Kelno's two personal bodyguards came bursting out of his private chambers. They were ready. One had his revolver drawn.

Boom! Dr. Cooper fired first with a blinding flash, and the gun went flying from the guard's hand. A boot hit the guard in the chest like a battering ram, and the other guard got a rib-cracking fist.

Five down.

In his chambers, Stuart Kelno jumped up from his breakfast. "What's—who are you?"

The mad invader took hold of the breakfast table and flipped it up, spattering Kelno's meal all over him and pinning him against the wall with a clatter of breaking dishes and a splintering of wood. An iron fist clamped onto Kelno's collar so he could not move, and then there was an ominous click.

Stuart Kelno was looking down the barrel of a cocked 357 Magnum, and right behind that barrel were the cold blue eyes of a very deadly, very angry, very unkillable enemy.

TWELVE

Kelno was speechless and visibly terrified. He could only stare and tremble, gasping for each breath, his eyes glued to those cold eyes.

The animal holding him did not say a word and did not loosen its grip for what seemed an eternity.

"Are you . . ." Kelno struggled to say, "are you back from the dead, Jacob Cooper?"

The big fist tightened its grip and a growling voice said, "Where is my daughter?"

Kelno knew he had no acceptable answer for that. "You—you are a Christian! You cannot kill me in cold blood!"

"My daughter!"

"You cannot kill me!"

Dr. Cooper lifted Kelno right off his feet with a powerful arm. "I can, Stuart Kelno. Right now, more than ever, I most certainly can."

Kelno believed he was about to die.

But then, as if Dr. Cooper had been startled by his own words, the cold, fierce eyes mellowed and the grip loosened just a little. The look of anger on Dr. Cooper's face melted to an expression of deep sorrow. A silent, terror-frozen moment passed, and then, with a mournful sigh, he turned the barrel of the gun safely away and returned the hammer to rest. He slipped the 357 back into its holster.

"You're not going to kill me?" Kelno asked, starting to feel relieved.

Dr. Cooper could not answer right away. He was too disturbed by his own actions.

"I . . . was about to," he finally replied. "Lila is dead because of you. I certainly could have taken your life."

"Why didn't you?"

"I gave Lila . . . I gave both my children to the Lord the day they were born. Even my own life doesn't belong to me. The Coopers belong to Jesus. He bought us with His own blood, and our lives are His to preserve . . . or to take."

Stuart Kelno was still very much aware of that immovable iron fist around his neck. "What are you going to do with me?"

"Vengeance belongs to God, not to me. You can answer to Him for what you've done. In the meantime, I'm going to pass God's grace along. Jesus saved *me;* I'm going to try to save *you.*" Dr. Cooper threw the table aside and then half carried Kelno toward the door. "Please hurry. This island is going under in a matter of hours."

They stepped out through the broken front door and onto the veranda. The fallen guards were just picking themselves up, still wondering what had hit them. The townspeople had heard the shot and the scuffle, and had come running.

"Hold it, everyone!" Dr. Cooper yelled, gripping Kelno very firmly.

They all kept their distance as they continued to gather in the square, their eyes filled with horror. What is this? A ghost? An immortal man? This invulnerable being who had twice cheated death now held their leader. Lord Kelno was at his mercy!

"There's a friend here who'd like to have a word with you," said Dr. Cooper, and then he looked across the square to where Adam came out of hiding and climbed onto a large rock. Jay stood below him with the two sheepish sentries.

The whole crowd gasped, looking at Adam and Jay, and then at Dr. Cooper, and then at Adam again. The same thing could be clearly read on all their faces: What is happening here? These men are back from the dead!

Adam spoke out clearly. "Friends! Many of you know me. Sam, Bernie, Joyce, Trudy, Jim, we've worked together, prayed together. You know how I came to this island to spread the good news of Jesus Christ, how He came to save us all and give us life. I'm still committed to that, and the invitation to find Him as Lord and Savior is still open. But listen to me: I also want to save your lives. You've heard the rumblings, you've felt the ground shaking, you've seen the signs, you've heard the warnings. Friends, I tell you the truth. This island is doomed. It's sinking beneath us at this very moment."

"Don't listen to him," Kelno shouted. "He cannot save you. Jesus cannot save you. You need no savior but yourself."

"I've built a boat!" Adam shouted. "If Stuart Kelno won't let you escape on his own craft, then I invite you to escape on mine. I offer this invitation to anyone who will accept it, but we must leave now."

"He's lying!" shouted Kelno. "I have the truth. This island will never sink. I will not allow it."

Adam responded, "The foundations of the island are being eroded away by the sea right now, as we speak. The core of the island is breaking up. It could collapse at any moment."

As if to underline Adam's words, the ground gave a

mighty shudder and several people fell down. A dangerous panic was sweeping over the crowd. They began to stir about and talk excitedly among themselves.

"Silence!" shouted Kelno. "Silence! I am lord here! You will do as I say!"

"Then stop the earthquakes," an elderly man shouted.

"Who said that?" Kelno demanded angrily, looking over the crowd.

But now several more shouts arose.

"Yeah, you said the quaking would stop. Well, it hasn't," said a housewife.

"Hey, I'm a geologist, and I think MacKenzie's right," said a well-dressed man.

"I don't want to die!" a young girl shouted.

The people were beginning to divide, some for Kelno, and some for Adam. The crowd was getting very restless, panicky, and nasty.

The rumblings grew worse. The ground quivered, the windows in the buildings rattled, the trees were swaying and trembling.

"We must leave immediately," said Adam. "Please come with me."

"Stay!" ordered Kelno.

But many ran to the rock where Adam was standing. Those still loyal to Kelno tried to pull them back, but they resolutely remained.

Dr. Cooper spoke to Kelno. "How about it? Between your boat and Adam's, we can get all these people safely off the island. We can save all of them."

"This is our home. Our new world. *We* hold the future."

"You have no future here. Don't be foolish! You can be saved, you and all your followers."

Kelno saw that soon the people would be out of his

control. He raised his hands and shouted, "Everyone listen to me!" The crowd quieted. "These men are liars, and you must not fear them. This gospel, this talk about Jesus, is only a deception, something to destroy your faith in your own power. There is no savior except yourself. Why turn to them or to their God for salvation? *You* are all the God you need!"

"Yes," some shouted. "Lord Kelno is right. We can save ourselves."

"But what about the earthquakes?" someone else wanted to know.

"What earthquakes?" Kelno mocked. "I say they are nothing but an illusion, something you've all conceived in your own frightened minds."

The timing could not have been better. Suddenly, as the earth gave a mighty lurch, the dining hall up the hill from the village square creaked and groaned. Then, with a mighty sound of ripping boards, crumbling brick, and shattering glass, it tore right down the middle like a phone book in the hands of a strongman! Everyone screamed, but the excitement did not end there. With a deep rumble and a long, loud rrrrip, a black, jagged crack zig-zagged down the lawn in front of the dining hall, yawning and stretching until it tore into the square. People scrambled out of the way as the village was sliced right through the center as if with a huge, invisible knife.

Adam grabbed the chance. "Come with me! Let's leave right away!"

Families ran after him, some college professors ran after him, some laborers leaped over the deep, still-widening crack to follow. And all the screaming and yelling and threatening that Stuart Kelno could muster would not bring them back.

The island was shaking relentlessly now, and Dr.

Cooper could see no further reason to stick around. He let go of Kelno, who lost his balance from all the shaking and fell to the veranda floor.

"If you'll excuse me," said Dr. Cooper. "Jay, let's get out of here!" Dr. Cooper leaped over the growing crack, and he and his son followed the fleeing crowd out of the village.

Kelno struggled to his feet and braced himself against a post on the veranda. Enraged, he shouted to his remaining followers, "These men are devils, and they mock me! After them! Destroy them all!"

His loyal sentries and right-hand men took up the call, banded themselves together, and picked up their weapons. They chased the escaping throng, leaping over that widening crack and running in wild, swerving patterns as the quaking ground reeled like a storm-tossed ship.

Lila and Candle ran up the hill and into the supply-filled hut, and then down the hill with boxes, and then up again, and then down. They were frantically loading goods into a very large dugout canoe Candle had tied up at the shore where the village once stood. They slipped and staggered, but they kept at it. The ocean was starting to boil, and the waves were getting high and violent. It seemed the whole world was coming apart.

"Go!" yelled Candle, urging both of them to hurry. "We go plenty!"

They ran into the supply hut. Lila grabbed two cans of gasoline. Candle picked up what looked to him like a box of muffins, popping one into his mouth.

Lila saw it just in time. "No, Candle, no!"

He made a horrible face and spit it out. She caught it before it hit the ground.

"No," she said. "This isn't food. This is plastic explosive. Bad stuff! Plenty bad stuff!"

"Bad stuff," Candle agreed, putting the box back.

"So this is why the boat didn't explode when they burned it. Candle, you're a real blessing," she laughed.

"Go! We go plenty!" was his only response, grabbing a box of real food.

They took their last load down to the big canoe, and then, jumping in and grabbing their paddles, they pushed away from the rapidly sinking shore. They pulled on the paddles with all their strength, but of course Candle with his huge arms did most of the propelling. He kept hollering at Lila, though, so she continued paddling as best she could. They headed out past the worst waves and then turned to follow the shoreline.

"How far is it to the tunnel entrance?" Lila called to Candle.

"Adam, you papa, not far. We get there, you see," Candle shouted over the roar of the quaking island and the violent dashing of the waves.

The canoe fought its way through the pounding surf. They were getting wet, but they kept pulling.

Adam reached the clearing and the Pit. He motioned to his new escapees to climb down the rope, at which they immediately stalled.

"It's how we got up here," he explained. "Please hurry."

Dr. Cooper and Jay introduced themselves, learned people's names, and helped them climb down. "Pleased to meet you. Hang on now, Mary. Chuck, put your foot there, right. Not too fast, Cindy. Ed, grab onto that root there."

"What about that monster down there?" somebody asked.

"Trust the Lord," said Dr. Cooper.

The canoe kept knifing through the waves and Lila kept paddling, trying to help Candle. Off to their side, the shoreline was being eaten up by the sea: tall palms were marching, row upon row, into the surf, flopping forward into the waves. A huge slab of volcanic rock sheered away from a hillside and thundered into the sea, sending up a monstrous column of white water.

Lila could feel doubts and fears rising in her, but she kept paddling. Maybe . . . maybe her dad and Jay were all right. Maybe there really was a tunnel somewhere.

The lanterns were lit. Adam kept one in front of the line, and Jay had one at the other end. Dr. Cooper led the way with Adam, trying to remember which was the right path down through this maze of tunnels, cavities, and cracks. So far they had made the right turns.

Up above, sixteen armed men clustered around the Pit and stared aghast into the hole.

"Down *there?*" one asked, dumbfounded. "You gotta be kidding!"

"Hey," said another, "I'm a believer in the cause, but . . . well . . ."

"Why go after them? They're as good as dead already."

But then they heard the shrill voice of Stuart Kelno behind them. "What are you waiting for? Move! I will not be mocked in the presence of my followers!"

"What about the Serpent?" the group leader asked.

Kelno seemed sure of himself as he said, "Don't worry. He has been appeased. He has already had his meal."

It was either go into the Pit or face Stuart Kelno's wrath. In single file the men grabbed the rope and started down.

Adam, the Coopers, and their precious twenty-seven had reached that horrible rift that had cut the tunnel in half. The two walls were still moving, shuddering, shifting in and out like two chewing jaws. Adam's adrenalin was really pumping; with a running leap he bounded across the chasm, landing and tumbling on the other side. He caught the rope tossed to him by Dr. Cooper and secured it around a rock formation. Dr. Cooper secured his end the same way, and now they had a safety rope.

"C'mon, Joe, you can do it!" Dr. Cooper shouted, and the others rooted for the former business executive as he took a running jump and cleared the chasm.

Now he turned and encouraged his wife and son, and they went for it. The walls closed just enough. They both made it across.

"Go, Randy!" they all yelled, and the young carpenter made it.

"Steady, Chuck!" they shouted, and Chuck crawled hand over hand along the rope to where many hands could finally grab him.

He was followed by some families and some single folks. One little girl was too small and too terrified to jump, so her father inched his way along the rope with her clinging to his chest. They made it.

Jay leaped across, landing less than a toe's length

from the edge. But there were plenty of waiting arms to grab and pull him in.

Finally Dr. Cooper was the only one left. The rope had to go with the group, so he untied his end and then secured it around his waist.

"C'mon, Doc!" everyone cheered from the other side.

"Take up the slack!" Dr. Cooper shouted, and Adam grabbed the other end of the rope and directed some other men to help him pull the rope tight.

The ground gave a mighty lurch. Almost everyone fell to the floor of the tunnel or against the walls. They could feel the island dropping under them.

Dr. Cooper knew better than to wait. He ran as fast as his powerful legs could carry him, took a flying leap from the edge of the chasm . . .

No! The wicked chasm was yawning open again, and the opposite ledge was moving away from him! His feet struck the opposite wall several feet below the ledge, and then his body fell backward, plunging head-first into the chasm.

The rope whistled and whirred over the rocky edge in a blur, and before Adam even knew what was happening it yanked him off his feet, onto his stomach, and then headfirst over the edge. The two men behind him were flat on the rocky floor of the tunnel, their palms burned, before the rope finally snapped taut, still tied to the rock formation on that end.

Dr. Cooper was several feet down, hanging by the rope around his waist, trying to recover from his body slamming against the wall and the rope practically cutting him in half. Adam was right above him, dangling and hanging on with a determination only the Lord could give him.

There was no time to speak or think. The island's core was shifting and wrenching, and the chasm would not hold still. The walls groaned and swayed back and forth, in and out. Then, much to the horror of everyone, they began inching together again. The chasm was closing up!

Jay and the faithful twenty-seven began to shout frantically and pull on the rope. Dr. Cooper dug his feet into the wall and tried to work his way upward. The rocks broke off under his feet and plummeted into the rift, bounding from wall to wall to wall to wall to wall and finally landing with a distant splash.

"Pull!" everyone shouted.

The rope inched upward. Adam came within reach and they pulled him to safety.

The rumble was increasing. The walls kept shifting and closing, releasing loose fragments that fell around Dr. Cooper's head. They swayed in two feet, out two feet, in two feet, out one foot, in three, in another two.

Dr. Cooper tried to reach up and grab the ledge. He couldn't

The walls were closing faster now.

"Pull!"

The rope inched upward. Dr. Cooper dug in with his feet again and pushed himself up. The chasm was eight feet wide. Six.

Dr. Cooper reached up with his hand and several hands grabbed it.

Four feet wide.

They pulled him out and he rolled onto the ledge.

Scrrrunchhh! With a thunderous grinding, a flurry of fragments, and billows of choking dust, the walls collided.

Dr. Cooper saw no reason whatsoever to wait around. "Show's over! Let's go!" he shouted, leaping to his feet and herding everyone down the tunnel.

* * *

"Candle!" Lila shouted, turning her head to avoid a violent splash of seawater. "How much further?"

Candle was not looking well. His eyes darted this way and that, his face etched with concern. He looked lost.

"Candle?" Lila asked again.

He stammered, and even whimpered a little, muttering several frantic sentences in his own language.

The canoe was rocking and filling with water as the angry, boiling sea splashed over them. The ocean was still swallowing the island and the ground sunk lower and lower like a torpedoed ship. Huge pieces were breaking off and crashing into the waves, turning the surf a muddy brown. The surrounding ocean was beginning to move inward as if sucked down a hole. Candle and Lila were caught in the pull of the current, and they tried to paddle against it.

The fleeing party finally broke through into the vast cavern under the island, but it was not the same cavern Adam and the Coopers had left. The river had swelled to a storm-tossed muddy sea, with waves dashing and crashing against the walls of the cavern and rock formations collapsing into the angry water with tremendous splashes of mud and foam. Adam's little camp was gone, washed away as if it never existed.

"The boat!" Adam cried.

There it was, no longer on its blocks, but afloat, rocking on the muddy, boiling water. They clambered down the side of the cavern to the water's edge. Adam leaped into the dirty brown soup and swam for his boat. When he reached it, he grabbed the side and pulled himself up and in. He found a good length of rope and tossed the end to Dr. Cooper, who caught it and then, with the help of several men, pulled the wild, bucking boat in toward the edge.

"Careful, don't let it hit the rocks."

Several men waded into the water to steady the big tub. One by one, the men, women, and children waded through the water and clambered into Adam's Ark.

Adam had a large outboard motor bolted to the back. He cranked it up, and the old hulk began to move through the water.

The roaring, crunching, and grinding of earth, rock, and water filled the cavern. The ceiling began to shower pebbles, dust, boulders, and fragments down on them, landing all around the boat, sending up columns of water like exploding artillery shells. There was nothing to do about that but pray.

Adam headed the Ark toward where the tunnel was supposed to be, but as the light from their lanterns continued to probe into the darkness he was steadily overcome with a horrible fear.

"The water . . ." he said. "The water's too high!"

Ping! A splinter of wood seemed to explode from the boat's railing and plop in a woman's lap.

Ping! Bam! Thud!

"Get down!" Dr. Cooper yelled.

Yes, those were gunshots. Kelno's men had reached the cavern! The Ark's passengers looked back and saw about a dozen lights sweeping about in the cavern.

"Do you see the tunnel?" Dr. Cooper asked.

Adam held a lantern high; he shined a flashlight this way and that. Then his face went pale, and his jaw trembled.

"We've reached the archway," he said. "But . . . but the island has sunk too far!"

Candle threw back his head and screamed—a mournful, anguished sound. He held his head in his hands, he trembled, he shook his head, he screamed again.

Lila looked around. She saw the roaring, quake-stirred water, and the mud, and the floating debris from the doomed island, and the rocky cliffs above them, but she saw no tunnel.

"Candle!" she cried. "What's wrong?"

He cried out and pointed down toward the water.

"What?" asked Lila. "What are you saying? Where's the tunnel?"

Candle cried out again, weeping, and pointing down at the water again.

Lila tried to hang on to her hope, but now she realized. "Down—down there? *Under* the water?"

"We're trapped!" Adam cried.

More shots rang out. They had nowhere to duck, nowhere to go. The probing light beams were seeking them out, and the armed men were coming closer, working their way along the steadily shrinking banks of this growing, angry caldron.

Dr. Cooper looked up. "The water's still rising! Look! We're coming up toward the ceiling."

Adam shined his flashlight straight up, and the rough, black-rock ceiling was pressing steadily downward like a descending cloud.

"We'll be crushed!" he said.

"Mommy," said a little girl, "my ears hurt."

Dr. Cooper agreed. "The air pressure is increasing. The lava vent must be sealed up now. The water's coming in, but the air can't get out."

"And neither can we," said Adam.

More shots rang out. The bullets ripped into the boat. Chips of wood fluttered through the air.

The water kept rising. That black, rocky, crushing ceiling was relentlessly lowering.

THIRTEEN

Candle and Lila pulled on the paddles for all they were worth, and the canoe fought its way through the waves and out away from the island's crumbling, muddy mass. They had to get clear before they were sucked down, gobbled up by the churning sea. Candle was frantic and babbling, not knowing what to do next.

"Pray, Candle!" Lila shouted. "Pray! God will show us what to do!"

He was praying all right; his words tumbled out like a bag of marbles.

Lila prayed too. "Lord God . . . I need an idea. I'll take anything You have."

Suddenly there was a crash, and Lila and Candle jumped with a start. From nowhere, a large chip of volcanic rock fell into the canoe, smashed a case of canned goods, and broke into two jagged halves that came to rest in the bottom of the canoe.

Candle cried out in fear and pulled on his paddle with powerful strokes. He didn't want to be hit by any flying rocks.

Lila felt the same way, and paddled desperately.

"Lord," she prayed, "I didn't ask for *that!*"

Or did she? Her eyes widened, and her mouth dropped open. She stopped paddling, turned around, and took another look at the jagged piece of rock now at her feet. She reached down with trembling fingers to feel its surface, and then picked it up. It was light and brittle, and it was giving her an idea. With enough force this type of rock could possibly be made to crack, to shatter.

"Candle," she asked, "remember what you told me about the cavern?"

He understood her a little, but his main concern was that she had stopped paddling, and he made his usual wild gestures to get her to pick up her paddle again.

"Candle, listen to me!"

He was listening.

"The cavern—" she said, making gestures to clarify her meaning. He understood. "Is it all made of *this?*" She pointed at the piece of rock.

Candle nodded, and indicated with a wave of his arms that the entire cavern—floors, ceiling, and walls—was made of this same black, volcanic rock.

It had to be the Lord; Lila was feeling a new strength and courage flowing through her. She grabbed her paddle.

"C'mon, let's row!" she shouted. "We've got to get back to your supply hut before it sinks!"

Down under the doomed island, in the rapidly shrinking cavern, the angry waters kept rising, pushing the helpless old Ark higher and higher toward the ceiling.

"We'll be crushed!" Adam cried.

Ping! Pow! Kelno's ever-loyal henchmen were still firing at them. The helpless passengers could only huddle in the bottom of the boat and pray that the bullets would miss.

"Hold your fire!" Dr. Cooper yelled. "We can't get out. You have us."

The trigger-happy pursuers liked that news. They quit firing, thank the Lord, and started running toward the boat along the rocky banks of the tossing and angry lake, the beams of their lights sweeping through the cavern.

"Bring the boat in," one of them yelled.

"All right," Dr. Cooper shouted back. "Just don't shoot."

"What can we do?" Adam whispered.

"What can *they* do?" Dr. Cooper countered.

Indeed, those proud and haughty henchmen were just now starting to wonder that very thing. Yes, they'd captured the boat full of fleeing refugees, but now what? All around them the cavern was quaking, crumbling, and caving in. Moreover, the lava vent they had followed to get here was now completely blocked. There was no getting out! The sixteen men stood still on a narrow shelf of rock above the water and began to search about the rest of the cavern for some other way out of this trap; the light beams swept to and fro, desperately trying to spot anything that might bring a glimmer of hope.

Then the shelf broke off. Eight men, then two more, and finally twelve of the sixteen fell headlong into the brown waves, screaming and splashing in desperation. The remaining four clung to the rocks like feeble flies, with nowhere else to go but into the threatening lake.

Dr. Cooper led the way as he jumped over the side of the boat and swam toward the struggling men. Adam joined him, as did Joe the executive and Randy the carpenter. Kelno's men had lost their fight by now, and were willing enough to be hauled aboard the boat. Their guns had fallen to where they belonged—the bottom of the rising water.

"Come on aboard," said Adam, helping them one by one.

"What's going to happen?" they wanted to know. "Are we going to die?"

"The one true God only knows," said Dr. Cooper, watching as the boat continued to inch upward toward the ceiling, while falling boulders and fragments splashed all around them. Everyone could feel the pain in his ears as the air pressure continued to build.

Candle and Lila manuevered the canoe between the half-sunken palm trees, past rooftops of the rapidly disappearing huts, and right up to the supply hut, now being threatened by the foaming surf lapping and dashing at its very door. All around them the palms were whipping and whistling through the air in wild arcs, and the ground was rocking, cracking, and crawling as if liquified.

Lila decided not to think about it. Other things were too important. She leaped from the canoe and into the swirling, muddy water, pulling the boat onto the steadiy dissolving land. Then, with a grim, firmly-settled determination, she dashed into the tottering supply hut and started ripping open crates. Candle, almost crazy with fear, followed her, shaking his head and muttering words of doom.

Lila was filling a knapsack with the foul-tasting "muffins" Candle had almost eaten. He stood behind her, watching with fascination and wonder.

"Bad stuff?" he asked.

"Very bad stuff," she answered, still grabbing up

the small round globs. "Can you reach that box up there?"

He brought the box down for her. She started counting out as many of the small, timed detonators as she thought she would need.

"Candle," she said, "draw me a picture." She pointed to the dirt floor. "Show me what the cavern looks like. The whirlpool." She made the sound of the whirlpool, and he nodded his head.

As Lila continued counting detonators and wads of explosive, Candle stooped and scratched out a diagram in the dirt. She then studied it carefully.

"That wall there—" she said, pointing. "The wall, the one between the whirlpool and the cavern . . . How thick is it? How much rock?"

It took her a few moments and a few gestures to get her meaning across, and it took him a few dashes back and forth across the hut to show her how thick the wall was.

"Much wall," he said, shaking his head. "Plenty rock!"

"More muffins," said Lila, digging some more out of the crate and putting them in her knapsack. She ended up taking them all.

Her last item was a small emergency bottle of oxygen with a breathing tube and mouthpiece. She strapped that to her waist.

"What . . . what you do?" Candle wanted to know.

"Candle," she said, pointing toward the rising shoreline, "better pull the canoe up further."

He looked, and she was right, so he ran down to take care of it.

Lila ran up the trail. She couldn't let him know what she was about to do. She couldn't let him stop her.

* * *

On the other side of the island, men, women, and children screamed in despair as they stopped short on a trail toward the water. They had come expecting to find a dock, but now there was none. They were hoping to escape the island in Stuart Kelno's boat, but it was destroyed, lying in ripped and bent pieces under a terrific landslide of rocks and trees. It was too late. Now there was no escape.

"We're going to die!" screamed one of Kelno's guards as he lay in the bottom of the rocking, tossing, mud-spattered boat. "We're going to—"

Dr. Cooper's hand clamped over his mouth. "Be still. You're upsetting everybody."

Adam could see the ceiling coming steadily down as the waters kept rising.

Soon there would be little of the open cavern left. "Isn't there something we can do?" he kept asking.

"I think we'd better be sure all these people are ready to . . . meet the Lord," said Dr. Cooper.

Adam nodded, and stood in the boat to lead them all in a prayer. They all prayed with him. Not one refused.

Lila stood on a towering cliff of rock, on the very spot where the bridge had been, and looked down into the angry throat of the whirlpool. It was still fierce, horrible, monstrous, and spinning like a huge vertical tunnel. She knew that in just a few seconds she would be too petrified to continue—she would lose her nerve and crumble into a helpless, very useless, whimpering wreck. If Jay and her father were still alive down there, she would be no help to them at all. It would take a good, fast run to clear the rocky cliff and sail out over that hungry monster's mouth. She ran back to a good starting point.

Lila, said a voice inside her, *this is absolutely crazy. You'll be killed!*

"Lord Jesus, help me!" she cried.

She could feel the panic starting: her stomach was curled up tightly inside her, her hands were beginning to shake, her breath was coming in quivering gasps, her fingers were numb with terror. She could hardly hold the mouthpiece of her oxygen bottle to jam it into her mouth.

She called for the Lord's help again, her words garbled by the mouthpiece. Then she opened the valve. The air filled her lungs. She pulled the knapsack securely against her chest. She prayed one more time. She started to run.

One step, another, another, her feet pounding the rocky ground. The cliff was approaching. She ran harder. Only two more steps left. Only one!

The last was a giant leap. She sailed outward as the rocky ground dropped suddenly away. She felt like she was floating. She was screaming. The wind rushed past her, roaring in her ears. She could see the spinning tunnel about to swallow her up. She felt like *she* was spinning. The opposite cliff was a rushing blur of black and gray.

"Ooooooofff!"

The water felt like a marble floor. She plunged under, and the mouthpiece tore from between her teeth in a cloud of bubbles. Cold, dirty seawater gushed into her mouth like a fire hose. She felt crushed like an insect. Then she saw nothing, felt nothing, thought nothing.

Time passed. It could have been seconds, it could have been minutes. She recovered her senses. She was tumbling and spinning in all directions, trapped in a cyclone of roaring water and debris, her arms and legs flailing outward. She was drowning. Madly she groped about her body for that mouthpiece. *Lord, help me!* There! She got it and with great effort jammed it into her mouth. The first breath of oxygen reinflated her lungs, and the kinks came out of her rib cage with rippling shock waves of pain.

I must be alive, she thought. *The pain's about to kill me!*

She opened her eyes to dim, brown light. The water was murky, but she could see a rocky, underwater surface rushing by not too far away. She could sense that direction was up. She must be moving under the wall, swept along by the current. She paddled with her arms. The rocky surface came closer.

She reached out and grabbed it. Now the current was trying to tear her loose.

There wasn't much time. Her oxygen was only good for a few minutes. She reached into the knapsack on her chest and pulled out a wad of explosive. This might be a good place, or it might not be, but why not? She had plenty, and a little overkill wouldn't hurt. She jammed the wad into a crack in the rock, attached a detonator, and set the timer for five minutes, then turned a small timer on her wrist to five minutes. She let the current carry her a few more feet until she grabbed onto the rocks again and planted another wad and detonator.

Okay, she thought. We'll see how many of these I can plant before I run out of time, or run out of charges or run out of *air!*

The kingdom of Stuart Kelno was coming to a horrible end. The dining hall was a pile of rubble, gobbled up from the middle outward by the ever-growing fissure in the earth. All around the village, windows were breaking out and roofs were collapsing as the houses twisted and contorted, their doors flapping back and forth like flags in the wind. The ground was heaving and rolling like a stormy ocean.

The people who had remained, those loyal followers of a false messiah, were now screaming in terror and running here, there, then back again. They were fleeing the deadly cracks that continued opening up throughout the village and dividing the roads, splitting the houses, even tearing apart the trees. The quaking ground was like slow mud as it oozed and shifted. The trees whipped back and forth, touching the ground on one side and then the other, until they finally snapped like toothpicks and flopped down on houses and storage sheds.

Stuart Kelno remained near his cottage, no longer able to control his people. He figured there was nothing to do now but wait for this horrible shaking to stop—oh, and it *would* stop, he was sure—so the rebuilding could start.

But then he heard a loud snap and the swish of palm branches through the air, and looked just in time to see a huge palm tree flop down on his cottage, cutting it neatly in half. Wood, glass, idols, and books flew everywhere. How could this be? A tree falling on the house of a *god?* Suddenly Kelno began to feel small and helpless; if he *was* a god or if he did have divine control over the forces of this island . . . it was getting harder and harder to believe it.

He looked this way and that. His followers were scattering in all directions. No one was watching him. A thought occurred to him. Perhaps the missionary was right all along. Perhaps there was still some room on that boat of his.

Kelno tried to look cool and in control, but he

began to make his way swiftly through the village, dodging opening fissures, falling trees, and frantic people, heading toward that jungle trail.

Let them all die, he thought. *I will live!*

The pain in the ears of every person on that doomed little boat was excruciating, and it was becoming very difficult to hear. The ceiling, that savage, merciless, black, rocky ceiling, was still coming down upon them like the jaw of a huge nutcracker.

Dr. Cooper put his arm around Jay and held him close. Neither one spoke. What was there to say? There was every likelihood in the world that they were going to die, and they were now trying to resign themselves to that fact.

Adam kept on praying with everyone. "Do you know Jesus?" he would ask. "Are you ready to meet Him?"

Lila continued paddling against the current and jamming wads of explosives into strategic cracks wherever she could find them. There would be quite a show when all these charges went off.

She was working her way from one side of the passage to the other, finding a crack here, a crevice there, a potentially weak spot a little further on. She could only hope she was doing it right. She kept her eye on her little wrist timer. In one minute, the charges would detonate.

No! What was this? The rocky surface just above her suddenly started dropping, making a horrible noise that carried through the murky water like thunder. A huge piece of the wall had broken loose and was coming down right on top of her! She paddled like a maniac, trying to wriggle her way out from under this sinking, crushing mass of stone.

It caught her! It was pushing her down. Lila crawled along its belly toward the edge, trying to get around it. The water was rushing around her, and the pressure was increasing. She thought she had crawled clear when the big slab hit the bottom of the passage with a rumbling crash. Pain shot through her left leg. She kicked to get away.

Oh no! Her leg was pinned under the edge of the slab. She pulled, she struggled, but her leg was clamped under that stone as if held between huge, black teeth.

Lila looked at the timer on her wrist. She had thirty seconds.

FOURTEEN

Stuart Kelno finally stumbled and struggled his way through the quaking, reeling jungle to the sacred clearing. The altar stones had toppled, and the clearing was criss-crossed with fallen trees, but the Pit was still there, its yawning mouth inviting him in. He took hold of the rope the others had used, and tried to build up the nerve to proceed.

Candle had searched everywhere for Lila. He'd reached the precipice over the whirlpool, but she wasn't there; he'd run toward Kelno's village and back again, but didn't find her; he'd hurried down one trail and up another, but she was gone.

Now he stood in the middle of the roaring, reeling, shaking jungle, holding onto a swaying tree and weeping, calling out "Mee-Bwah!" and then saying Lila's name over and over.

Lila's lungs were empty. She sucked on the mouthpiece, but there was nothing left. The oxygen had run out!

Twenty seconds. Lila tore a small corner off one of

the plastic charges, jammed a detonator into it, found a
niche in the slab that looked promising, and set the
detonator for five seconds.

She then stretched her body as far away from that
charge as she could, wrapped her arms around her
head and over her ears, and waited.

It was like she'd been hit by an underwater freight
train. The sound was deafening, the concussion stun-
ning; the blast rattled her teeth. She was shooting
through the murky water like a torpedo, surrounded
by foaming, roaring bubbles and pulverized rock. She
was tumbling, her body limp, half-conscious, end over
end.

She couldn't feel her leg. Had she blown it off?

Only ten seconds left. She could feel the pressure
of the water easing. She was approaching the surface,
but where?

Five seconds.

Her head broke through into beautiful, delicious,
God-given air! She gasped it down and started swim-
ming. Now she could feel her left leg. Praise God—it
was still there, but it wasn't working. Dull, agonizing
pain shot through it. She'd broken something, maybe a
lot of things.

She grabbed for a rocky ledge, pulled herself up,
and rolled onto the shelf. There was a pocket in the
rocks, a little pool. She rolled into it for cover.

The people in the boat could touch the ceiling easily. Soon they would be against it.

Then it happened! The lake near the wall heaved
and blossomed out in all directions like one immense
flower of muddy water. A huge wave rolled outward,
racing along and slapping the walls of the cavern like a
monstrous brush. Hot stones of all sizes soared across

the room like comets and pounded the opposite walls like cannonballs.

The people in Adam's Ark didn't know what was happening. They only ducked as the wave washed over them, and they cowered as the stones pelted the boat and the lake.

The wave almost carried Lila away with it, but she kept herself anchored in her little pocket until it had washed over her. She looked up at the wall. It was still there.

Another explosion! The lake heaved up in another giant blast of foam, stones, and spray. More rocks shot out and sailed across the room. But the wall stood firm.

A third explosion! A fourth! A fifth! The shock waves rattled the cavern like the inside of a bell, jolting Lila several inches off the surface as she winced in pain.

Then she thought she heard a loud, cracking sound. She tried to see where it came from.

Still another blast!

There! Now she could see cracks forming in the wall. They were inching upward into the ceiling. Light shone through them in some places. The wall's supports had been blasted away. It was crumbling.

A final blast. The cracks widened and then, like a tremendous rockslide, like a collapsing curtain of huge, black cinders, the wall and a huge section of the ceiling disintegrated into fragments and dust and thundered into the lake. A filthy, towering wave of water, gravel, and silt washed over Lila.

The people in the Ark suddenly felt they were in a falling elevator. The surface of the lake dropped right out from under them, and the ceiling disappeared into the haze and spray high over their heads. The boat fell so fast that they almost came up off the floor. Then they saw light. The boat was moving through the cavern at tremendous speed, for the lake was pouring out of the cavern, like tea from a tilted cup, rushing with incredible force toward the light.

The entire side of the cavern had fallen in! They could see the sky up there and they were surging right for it!

Lila was floating helplessly in the lake that had now become a river, being swept along toward the daylight, toward that immense hole that used to be a wall. She could see the Ark now, not too far behind her, heading right toward her. She screamed, she waved. Did they see her?

"Grab her!" was all Dr. Cooper could say. He knew who it was, but there was no time to think about it. "Pull her aboard!"

The boat shot along the roaring rapids toward that opening as the lake cascaded out through it like a tidal wave. Lila paddled with very weak strokes against the current, trying to get to the boat. She was almost totally exhausted and numb with pain.

She saw the rough, wooden side, and then felt good strong arms grabbing her and lifting her out of the water. She flopped into the boat like a cold, dead fish.

"Look out!" Adam cried, and everyone ducked as the Ark shot through the opening, just barely squeezing under a very low ceiling. A jagged rock bit off a part of the stern as they passed.

But they made it! The cavern had belched them out like a cork from a bottle. The Ark was spinning and dancing on the surface of a boiling, rapidly rising column of water that filled the deep canyon where the whirlpool used to be. It was like sitting on top of a geyser. Now they were riding up in an elevator as they watched the walls of the canyon dropping all around them.

The island seemed to react to that very great puncture through its heart. With a long, steady, agonized shudder, it began to drop into the sea. The waves raced inland, roaring and thundering around the hills, tearing away the plant life, sweeping away logs, brush, the remains of buildings, even large boulders. The ocean gobbled up the rest of Candle's old village; surf pounded up the trails and over the jungle. The trees disappeared under the foam and then became a part of it, washing and tumbling along in a devastating wall of water and debris. Nothing could stand before this horrible tide.

Stuart Kelno's village was there—and then it was not. The sea came from three different directions, four feet deep, then six, then ten, then twenty. The houses put up no resistance. The maintenance building became a raft for only a moment, and then dissolved into thousands of sticks and splinters. On three sides, walls of water converged and collided with a thunderclap where the village square used to be, sending up an explosion of water, spray, and whatever was left of the Kingdom of Aquarius.

In the jungle, Candle looked one way and saw a wall of trees, mud, and seawater crashing and foaming toward him; he looked the other way and saw the same thing. The surf was rolling over the top of the island like a thousand stormy breakers, kicking up a violent wind.

Candle ran the only direction left, toward the highest hill on the island as the sea steadily closed in on him, rolling and thundering at his heels.

Stuart Kelno had just reached the floor of the Pit when he thought he felt the whole island listing, settling to one side like a sinking ship. He could feel the shuddering, the final death throes. A blast of foul air shot out of the passageway at his feet. He could hear seawater rushing up from below.

Then terror shot through his heart like a sharp arrow. He was suddenly looking right into the huge, vicious, rage-filled eyes of the Serpent, the ever-hungry god of this pagan island. The tongue flicked at him; the big neck arched high above him. Kelno tried to back away, but was blocked by the hard, merciless, stone wall of the Pit.

"Great Serpent . . ." he cried, trembling, begging. "It is I, Stuart Kelno, Lord of the Island of Aquarius!"

The Serpent had no regard for this man, no matter what he said.

Kelno kept trying to inch his way back to the rope. "I . . . I have revered you! I have led your people in worship and sacrifice to you!"

The big tongue continued licking and flicking at him. The mouth began to open.

"Please!" Kelno begged. "You—you cannot eat *me!*"

He grabbed for the rope and started to pull himself up. The Serpent made one quick, lightning-fast lunge and grabbed him by the heel. Kelno's hands were torn from the rope. The Serpent threw its head back, and the big throat opened.

Stuart Kelno was gone in a gulp.

Only seconds later, gushing in from below and thundering down from above, the raging sea swallowed up the Serpent. Both false gods were gone forever.

The sea rose to the top of the canyon and then spilled over the rest of the island, carrying the helpless little Ark with it. Adam had the outboard motor running, but there was nothing they could do against this terrific rushing current. The sea was washing over the last remaining high places. The Ark was swept past hilltops, through the treetops, over the submerging jungle, like one more little piece of debris amid the floating pieces of the dying island.

The Ark's passengers spotted some survivors, floundering and struggling in the swirling mud and foam, clinging to logs and lumber, waving and crying out for help. Adam steered the boat their way and picked them up. Many casualties floated past like driftwood, but nothing could be done for them.

"Hey!" Jay shouted. "What's that over there?"

"Where?" asked Adam.

"Up in that tree!" Jay answered, pointing.

Adam looked, and then he burst out in a glorious "Praise the Lord! It's Candle!"

The big Polynesian was high in the top of a towering palm—except that now the top of that towering palm was only a few feet above the water. Candle still clung to it, submerged up to the waist.

Adam brought the old tub right alongside the big palm tree before Candle even noticed it.

"Candle!" he shouted, his hands outstretched.

Candle looked up and saw his old friend. After just a short moment of disbelief, those big teeth glimmered in the sun and Candle began to weep for joy.

"Adam!" he cried, tumbling into the boat and embracing the missionary. "Bless Mee-Bwah! Bless Mee-Bwah!"

There was no time to waste. Adam revved the outboard to full throttle, and the old tub began to move steadily along. The initial currents were subsiding. With God's help, they could get clear of the island before any more violent surges took place.

Dr. Cooper tried to check Lila's battered and bleeding leg, but his eyes kept blurring with tears.

"Are you okay, Dad?" Lila asked.

"I . . . couldn't possibly be better," he said, holding her close and kissing her forehead. "I have you back, sweetheart. I just couldn't ask for more."

Jay was working on the leg, but he was weeping as well, overcome by the goodness of the Lord. They were together again! They were alive!

"It's broken, Sis," he told Lila, applying a crude splint to her leg.

"In how many places?" she asked.

"Well," he said hesitantly, "more than one. Let's leave it at that."

Lila looked at her father and brother with fear in her eyes. "Will I be able to walk again?"

Dr. Cooper, the proudest father that ever was, looked at his daughter and said, "Honey, I'm thoroughly convinced that with God's help you can do *anything* you set your mind to!"

"Okay," she said simply.

They looked behind them at the boiling ocean now closing over the island that no longer was.

"It'll be just like it was never there," said Lila.

"And so suddenly!" said Jay.

"Just like the whole world," said Dr. Cooper.

"Ready or not, the Bible says it's going to end some-day." He shook his head as he watched the sea foaming and swirling over the vanished island. "But think of it! Think of all the people on that island who just weren't ready, who just wouldn't listen." The next thought grieved him deeply as he spoke it. "They've all per-ished. They're gone."

"Along with their false god," Lila said very soberly.

Dr. Cooper nodded. "Exactly as it will be in the end. The whole world will be under the control of one man, a false god, a lying messiah, a world ruler . . ."

"The Antichrist," said Jay. "Amazing."

"And just like these people, they'll think they've found the perfect world, the perfect future, the perfect religion, and they won't even consider that the end of the world and God's judgments are right at their door-step."

"Boy," said Lila, "I'm glad I know the *real* God!"

"It pays to know Him," Jay agreed.

"Which means we could all learn a lesson from Adam," Dr. Cooper concluded.

They looked, and of course there was Adam, going about his God-given business. He was greeting the new passengers, then opening his Bible and telling them about Jesus. If he could help it, they would all be born-again believers by the time they got out of this boat.

Far behind them, a murky, debris-strewn ocean fi-nally began to grow calm. Soon there would be no sign that any island had ever been there.

A few miles out from the island's grave, the Lord blessed them by letting them find Candle's canoe, adrift and still loaded with enough food and fuel to get them to the nearest civilized island. They knew they would survive. They were all saved, in more ways than one.